KAI TAYLOR IS MY ENEMY BOYFRIEND

RUMORS AND LIES AT EVERMORE HIGH #5

EMILY LOWRY

Cover Photography by
VITOR LIMA VIA PEXELS

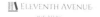 ELEVENTH AVENUE
PUBLISHING

A THANK YOU FROM EMILY

I wanted to take a moment to say thank you to my readers —
without you, none of this would be possible.

I truly appreciate every single review, Instagram post and
blog shout-out that you have given me. Every email, message
and kind word from you has brightened my day, every time.
You are the true MVPs!

To my ARC team, thank you for your endless encouragement
and incredibly helpful feedback. I value each and every
one of you.

For any of you who'd like to connect with me on social
media, you can find me on Instagram, Facebook and Tiktok -
I love nothing more than engaging with my reader community,
so please stop by and say hi!

Now, to write my next love story. Stay tuned!

Lots of love always,

XO, Emily

MAC

*T*he requirements to become Prom Queen were as follows:

You had to be popular.

You had to be beautiful.

You had to be a senior.

Okay, *technically* you could still win without being any of those three things. But it had literally never happened. And quite frankly, it never would happen. Not that I cared – the entire concept behind Prom King and Queen was archaic, classist, and borderline embarrassing.

We were in Evermore, not England. The closest thing America had to royalty was Beyoncé. So why did Evermore High go through the same prom ritual every year?

"Tradition. Plus, you know how much Evermore loves a cliché," Abby said. Abby was the editor at the school newspaper, and she'd been patiently listening to me rant for the last fifteen minutes. She scribbled in her notepad, then flipped it closed with practiced precision. "You should save this rant for your next article. Maybe if we take a shot at prom, people will actually read the Pinnacle."

Gold balloons and pink streamers stuck to the gym walls. A stage had been set up across from the bleachers. When their names were called, the "surprised" nominees would strut across the gym, take their place on stage, and blabber about what an honor it was to be nominated. A few months from now, two of the six nominees would be crowned King and Queen. Usually, it was the star football player and the head cheerleader... because why break with the cliché?

"If you want, I could write a rant about this gross misappropriation of school funds," I muttered, shifting on the bleachers. "We all know who the nominees are, so why bother with the assembly? How much do you think they spent on balloons, anyway?"

"Nothing compared to what they spend on the football program," Abby said. "But where's the fun in admitting how messed up this school is?"

I laughed, somewhat surprised that Abby was willing to take a shot at the football team. Her boyfriend was the legendary Chase Jones, all-state quarterback. They started dating in their junior year, and it had caused a huge stir on Click, Evermore High's gossip app. Quarterbacks weren't supposed to date nobodies. But then, along came Abby, proving everyone wrong.

Abby was one of the main reasons I signed on to work at the school newspaper this semester. Chase's sister, Jordyn, had overheard me ranting about school while I was visiting my best friend Sofia at Beachbreak Burgers. They thought my anger – scratch that – my *passion* would be a perfect fit for the paper.

"So what's the plan?" I asked.

"The gym will fill up soon and the assembly will begin. When Principal Potter announces the nominees, start taking notes. Look at their facial expressions, their body language. How much people cheer for them. Then, we'll pull them aside later this week to get their thoughts on being nominated. We'll see if we can cut through the stock responses. Jordyn and Hailey should be easy. Madison probably won't give us much. But maybe she'll smirk or something, and that might lead to a question about how confident she's feeling."

"Sneaky."

Abby grinned. "All the best journalists are."

"All the best journalists are what?" Chase Jones hopped up the bleachers, then sat behind Abby and hugged her.

Abby craned her neck to look at him. "Oh, you know… kind, caring, considerate. Perfect girlfriends who deserve to be lavished with gifts."

"Checks out." Chase tickled her ribs and she squealed.

I averted my eyes so I wouldn't have to see them kiss. They were so happy together it was almost gross.

"I'll meet you after the assembly for the interviews then, Mackayla?" Abby rose to her feet and slung her bag over her shoulder. "You'll interview the queens, I'll handle the kings."

"Sure thing."

Chase and Abby walked hand-in-hand across the bleachers to join their friends. Abby chattered animatedly as she bounced along, and Chase looked down at her in awe. Like she had solved world hunger or something. I'd never had an attractive guy — or any guy, for that matter — look at me like that.

Must be nice.

Slowly, students poured into the gym, swarming the bleachers. I scanned the crowd, looking for someone to sit with. Sofia, my best – and only – friend was at the other side of the gym with her boyfriend, Noah. I tried to make my way across, but I was swallowed by a wall of students, so I gave up and creeped to the back row of the bleachers. Out of sight, like a good journalist.

Also like someone who didn't have anyone to sit with.

"Coming to sit with me, Big Mac?" The voice belonged to the most obnoxious person at Evermore High – rising basketball star Kai Taylor. Who also happened to be my neighbor. My neighbor who constantly worked out shirtless, leaving his blinds open. He was also a constant pain in my butt. I dreaded the day one of his stupid nicknames would catch on.

"I'm working. Leave me alone."

"Don't be like that, Mac Daddy. Come sit with us." Kai gestured to an empty spot beside him. The rest of his pack – other basketball players and a handful of clingy girls – snickered.

I rolled my eyes. Sure, high school boys rolled in packs. They were like wolves, always following whoever the perceived alpha was. But the girls? Where was their sense of solidarity? Of girl power? Kai's ego was the size of Colorado – they didn't need to inflate it further by laughing at his lame jokes.

But that was Evermore. If you were a star athlete, you got everything handed to you.

And Kai, as much as I hated him, was a star. He was the only reason the basketball team was worth watching, and he was on track to single-handedly lead them to state.

"That one doesn't like me much," Kai said to one of the girls. "Well, she says she doesn't. But I've caught her peeking through the blinds. She likes to watch me when I work out."

Ugh. He was the worst. I shook my head. "Bite me, Taylor."

"See? Now she wants me to bite her." Kai blew me a kiss. "You're moving too fast for me, MacBook. You gotta take me out on a date first."

"As if I would ever willingly be alone in the same room as you." As deliberately as possible, I turned my back to him. Sofia always told me that I was overly offended by Kai because I secretly liked him. But that wasn't true. Kai was a jock. A poser. Popular only because he was good at throwing a stupid ball through a stupid hoop.

But I didn't care about that, and so I was completely immune to his athletic build, his angular jaw, and his dangerously playful smirk. Those dark eyes of his might have an effect on other girls, but not on me.

Ever.

I leaned back against the wall, kicking my scuffed Doc Martens out in front of me. Stupid, stupid Kai Taylor. One more year, and I'd be out of Evermore, away from all the cliques and the gossip and the drama.

One more year of fading into the background, unnoticed.

For now, I just had to focus on getting deets on the prom court nominees.

LIKE EVERYTHING else in Evermore High, the assembly was a long, overly pompous affair. Principal Potter, a squat, red-faced man who always wore mismatched socks, droned on about the recent success of the school basketball team. I noticed that he made no mention of our Model United Nations team taking second at regionals, or the Mathletes winning yet another trophy.

Athletics always came first at Evermore. Or maybe that was just America.

I hoped it wasn't worldwide.

As if to prove my point, Principal Potter announced the first two nominees for prom king: Chase Jones and Dylan Ramirez, the star quarterback and star running back, fresh off a state championship. They stood on stage with the sashes over their shoulders, neither looking like they were particularly interested in being up there. The third nominee wasn't an athlete, at least – it was the student body president, Ben Goldstein.

Once everyone had finally stopped applauding, it was time for queen nominations. The entire gaggle of cheerleaders in the front row perked up and surreptitiously fixed their hair. I didn't know why they bothered. Everyone knew the nominees would be Hailey, Madison and Jordyn.

"And our first nominee... Madison Albright," Principal Potter called, a fixed smile on his face.

Madison was a social media star and cheerleader. The boys at school said she was the hottest girl at Evermore High. The girls said she was mean, spoiled, vindictive and stuck up. She glided to the center of the room, smoothing her cheerleading skirt as she went. Her smile was big and pearly white, her eyes glittery and sharp.

She wanted this. Badly.

"The second nominee... Jordyn Jones."

Chase Jones's twin sister, Jordyn, skipped to her feet, her eyes sparkling with amusement. She was opinionated, loud, sassy. Popular because of who she was – not that she cared. I suspected the only reason she'd want to win prom queen would be to take it away from Madison. *That* was the kind of pettiness I approved of.

Jordyn took center stage and held her hand out to Madison for a high-five. When Madison rolled her eyes, Jordyn pretended to pout, but her pout was quickly replaced by a playful smirk. Tension simmered between them, and Madison took a half-step away.

Maybe covering the run-up to prom wouldn't be so boring after all.

I flipped open my notebook, trying to imitate the way Abby did it so I would look more professional. Instead of looking like a seasoned pro, my notebook slipped out of my hand and fell between the students in front of me.

"Sorry," I said, trying to reach between them. "If you could just pass that back…"

"Mackayla Lafelle."

I jerked my head up to try and figure out who said my name. "What?"

Frantic whispers broke out around the gym. Lots of people were looking at me.

"Mackayla Lafelle?" Principal Potter repeated, holding the microphone closer to his mouth.

"Sorry," I said. I held up my notepad. "Just dropped something. I'm ready now. Continue with the nominees."

The whispers around me turned into snickers.

"Mackayla? Could you please come to the stage?"

"Why would I do that?" I blurted.

There was a sharp, sudden laugh. Then Kai spoke. "Because you're the third prom queen nominee, Mac and Cheese!"

The snickers turned into full-blown laughter.

I was WHAT?

2

KAI

"Nineteen to sixteen," I said as I lined up for the shot.

Zane rolled his eyes. "It's sixteen to sixteen."

"Not after this shot." Shooting was all about confidence – owning the outcome of the basket before it even happened. You think LeBron ever took a shot thinking it wouldn't go in? No way. If you wanted to be a winner, you needed to think like a winner.

I feinted.

Zane leaped into the air in a last-second attempt at blocking the shot. I ducked underneath his arm, pivoted, and took my shot. The basketball arched through the air before sinking neatly into the net.

Swish. An easy three.

I looked over my shoulder at Zane. "Like I said – nineteen to sixteen."

"You got lucky, Taylor."

"Seems like I get lucky a lot when I play against you." I grabbed the ball, dribbled it between my legs, then tossed it to Zane. "Or maybe, you always throw yourself at every fake 'cause you're so desperate to stuff someone in the face. Now, do you want to pass me the ball so I can get to twenty-one and finish this up, or are you going to make me steal it?"

"I'm not giving you nothing," Zane snapped. He sounded angry, but he was smiling. Playing a little one-on-one with Zane before practice was usually the highlight of my day. He was the only person on our team who could keep up with me. During class, I felt slow, like I couldn't process everything going on around me. But when I was on the court, everything slowed down. Everyone moved in slow motion. Everything made sense.

And me? I was unbeatable.

"Catch me if you can, Taylor," Zane said. He tried to dribble past me and drive towards the basket, but I cut him off, keeping him to the outside. "Fine. I'll do it the hard way."

Zane lowered his shoulder and drove it into my chest. In a real game, it would've been a foul, but there weren't any real rules in twenty-one. I pretended to stumble. Zane lined up for the shot, but he was a breath too slow, and by the time he shot, I had already jumped in front of him and blocked the ball.

Aggressively.

It bounced off his forehead and right into my hands.

Zane looked around, bewildered.

"Over here, pretty boy," I said. Then, without breaking eye-contact, I took a no-look shot at the basket.

Swish.

"And that's game."

Zane flipped me off, but we were both laughing.

"Hey, Taylor, Coach wants to see you in his office!" Rob Altman, a sophomore teammate, called from across the gym.

"Cool," I replied. I tossed Zane the ball and jogged back to the locker room entrance, where Coach McMorris's office was located. I wasn't worried. I'd spent a lot of time with

Coach in his office, talking game play and college scholarship chances and even comparing our Fantasy picks. The basketball coach and I got along great — he was one of the only Evermore High staff members who seemed to like me.

I knocked on the door. "You wanted to see me."

"Get in here, Taylor," Coach barked.

Suddenly uncomfortable, I edged into the room.

Coach sat, stone-faced, behind his desk, clutching the edge of it with white knuckles. His eyes were stormy, and there was a vein in his temple that looked like it might burst.

He also wasn't alone. Mr. Vargas, my Video Game Production teacher was there, too. Vargas was a skinny, twitchy sort, who wore polka-dotted button downs and oversized glasses. He was a new teacher at Evermore this year, fresh out of Colorado State.

"What's up?" I asked.

Coach pointed to an empty chair. "Sit. Now."

I did.

"You're slacking, Taylor," Coach said.

"What? I'm at practice every day. And during lunch."

"There's more to life than basketball, Mr. Taylor," Mr. Vargas said. He opened his laptop and spun it to face me. "This is the project you turned in last week."

I gulped. I'd signed up for Video Game Production at the beginning of junior year, thinking it would be a joke class. In reality, it turned out to be a year-long nightmare of difficult coding I didn't understand. The project I'd turned in last week was a disaster.

I stared at the laptop screen, where a blue button prompted me to "PLAY".

"Indulge us, Mr. Taylor. Press the 'Play' button."

I clicked on the button. Nothing happened.

Mr. Vargas sighed like a disappointed parent. "Mr. Taylor, you were supposed to produce a simple, working puzzle game. 'Working' being the operative word. The game you submitted for your project doesn't even load. I have no choice but to give you an F."

"You can't do that," I blurted. "My dad will *kill* me."

"I don't decide your grade, Mr. Taylor. You did when you submitted yet another project that won't load." Mr. Vargas closed the laptop and shook his head. "Which, added to your list of very unimpressive grades so far this year, means you are now officially failing my class."

Failing?

I was *failing?*

Sure, I wasn't the best student in the class, but I'd never failed a class before. Especially not an elective. But why was Mr. Vargas telling me this now? At practice? In front of my coach?

"Evermore has a zero-tolerance policy for failure, Taylor. Remedial work and extra credit ain't going to cut it." Coach's stony expression darkened. "Until you get your grade up to a passing level, you're suspended from the team."

Coach shot Mr. Vargas an annoyed look, but I barely noticed the tension between the two men.

Suspended from the team?

SUSPENDED?

No. There had to be another solution. That wasn't how things were supposed to work around here.

I turned to Mr. Vargas, arranging my expression into the best remorseful plea I could muster. "Come on, man. You suspend me and we might not win another game. And forget about state."

"Athletes don't get special privileges in my class," Mr. Vargas said. "You have another assignment due tomorrow. If you get your grade up on that one, then you can be back on the team. Understood?"

The situation was so absurd I wanted to laugh. They were

willing to suspend their star basketball player because of a few bad assignments in an optional class that had no impact on my future. And, of course, it was the new teacher that did it. He was probably trying to make his mark.

"Understood," I muttered.

Coach stood, his face red. "Make this right, Taylor. ASAP. There's a game in three days, and I want you on the court."

"I will, Coach." I looked down at the ground, trying to hide how ashamed I was. "You can count on me."

I slunk out of the office. For as long as I could remember, basketball had been my escape from my admittedly mediocre academic performance. The court was the only place I felt like I belonged, the only place I felt like I knew what I was doing. And now, that was being taken away.

I shoved the gym doors open, almost smoking Hailey Danielson.

"My bad," I muttered. "You good?"

"Fine," she said. She raised her eyebrows. "You alright?"

"Never better."

The rest of the cheerleaders were behind her, ready for their own practice. They all looked at me, wide-eyed — today was a good day for the gossip they fed on like vultures.

The squad kept on staring at me until Hailey, their captain, waved them all away.

"Come on," she said, rubbing her temple. "Let's get moving, nothing to see here."

I tried to shoot Hailey a thankful look, but her back was already turned. Instead, I caught a glimpse of Madison Albright, stage-whispering to Lauren Cowley.

Her green eyes glittered as she hissed words that fanned the flames of my crippling shame.

"Kai Taylor's so dumb, he's getting suspended from the team for failing a video game class – like, how's that even possible?"

3

MAC

"Zombies on your six. Two runners and a bloater." As I spoke into my headset, my voice was cool and collected. Which was the exact opposite of how I felt after my prom queen nomination earlier today.

Who on earth thought it was a good idea to make me a prom queen nominee? I spent my life trying to avoid the spotlight, and now I was thrust on stage.

It was blatantly unfair.

"Take the shot, MickeyMac," one of my teammates replied.

"On it," I said. I adjusted my aim until the reticle fell over the three zombies chasing my teammate. Then, I started firing. There was nothing like destroying a few zombies to cheer me up. I fired, and the zombies chasing my teammate collapsed.

We were on a notoriously difficult level that was loosely based off of Dawn of the Dead. Our avatars were trapped inside a shopping mall, with zombies scrambling through the doors, the windows, and the vent. The objective was to find the seven keys you needed to unlock the door to the ceiling, where a helicopter was waiting.

Never mind that all of us had insanely powerful weapons that were more than capable of destroying the door. That was just video game logic. Though, I had mentally made a note that when I designed a game, I wouldn't use a cheat like that.

"MickeyMac, runner on you!"

"What? Where?"

"CEILING!"

I looked up—

And a green zombie with a wide gash where its mouth should've been fell on me.

I jumped, startled, and upset the dinner plate balancing on my lap so that I was now wearing my grilled cheese sandwich. Before I could process what had happened – both in the game and in real life – the zombie bit me, and it was game over.

"Got me." I sighed. "I'm out for the night, guys. Homework."

"GG."

"Good game," I said. I ripped off my headset, set my controller aside, and examined the mess I'd made. Liquid cheese had oozed all over my favorite t-shirt — black, with "I </Code> Like A Girl" written on the front.

"This isn't even the most disappointing thing that's happened today," I said to my t-shirt. I folded it over to prevent the cheese from dripping onto my floor, then made my way to the bathroom.

My little brother, Shaun, was in there, standing on a step stool in front of the mirror and examining his face.

"Whatya doing, buddy?" I turned on the faucet and wet a washcloth.

Shaun turned to me with all the solemness a nine-year-old could muster. "Did you know that the average adult human being has around 300 million skin cells?"

I shook my head. "I didn't. That's very interesting, though."

Shaun nodded, the weight of the world on his skinny little shoulders. "Also, a single square inch of skin has about 19 million cells and up to 300 sweat glands. My book says that you shed up to 40,000 dead skin cells per minute. But I've been looking in the mirror for eight minutes now, and I can't see anything."

I lifted the hem of my shirt and scrubbed the cheese stain. "Ah, buddy. I think that skin cells are really small. So small, you probably just can't see them with your eyes."

Shaun looked at me seriously. "So, with a microscope then?"

I had no idea. But I nodded anyway.

"Cool!" He yelled, running from the bathroom. Probably to go locate a microscope and put my theory to the test.

I hoped I was right. But at least I'd temporarily averted a classic Shaun meltdown. Which could occur over everything from polar ice caps melting to the theory that vegetables could feel pain.

I moved closer to the bathroom mirror, and as I was scrubbing my shirt in the sink, my phone bleeped.

It was Click.

Ugh. Why did I keep that stupid gossip app on my phone? I guess when you were as unpopular as me, and were never featured, it was easy to be a voyeur. Today, that changed. After my surprising nomination, I got a million messages and tags. People making fun of my deer-in-headlights expression, people questioning if I even went to Evermore, and, the most irritating – people making fun of my clothes.

My quirky, individual way of dressing was my small way of rebelling against Evermore's norms. And I liked how I dressed, even if it was too punk rock for high school. But… it was always uncomfortable being in the spotlight.

I swiped open my phone, bracing myself for the worst. I could take being called a Gwen Stefani wannabe or a vampire one more time today. Their words couldn't hurt me.

But the blast wasn't about me.

Evermore, could today get any juicier? Turns out that one all-star point guard has been slacking in his classes, and now he might get kicked off the team. The class he's failing? Video Game Production. That's right – Kai Taylor is failing an elective. Maybe he should spend less time flirting and more time studying. Or, maybe he's just a pretty face and nothing more. Cast your vote below!

Beneath a picture of Kai chatting to some girl was a poll. You could swipe left to say he should spend more time studying, or swipe right to say he was just dumb.

I didn't swipe.

I didn't like Kai one bit — Click was right that he was a slacker and a flirt who only got A's in Charm & Rugged Good Looks class. But after being featured on Click all day, I was feeling a bit more empathy for the popular kids who lived this reality permanently. Click was savage, a tank of piranhas waiting to tear into each victim.

And somehow, if it was even possible, Click had gotten worse. For as long as I could remember, Click had always felt random, like it had no unifying purpose other than to cause the maximum amount of drama. But, in the past few weeks, it was downright vicious. It felt like something had changed.

I was probably just being paranoid.

Besides, knowing Kai, he wouldn't care. He'd just use a Click blast like this to gain sympathy points with the ladies.

Me excluded, of course.

I wandered back to my bedroom and took a seat at my desk, my eyes flickering instinctively out my window. My bedroom window looked directly into Kai's, a fact that had tortured me daily since the Taylor family moved in last year.

Any time Kai was in his room, he was either working out shirtless or laying on his bed, texting with a goofy grin on his face. He never appeared to do homework. So, I didn't feel too bad for him — Evermore was finally asking its athletes to conform to the same academic rules as all of us mere mortals.

This afternoon, my stealthy glance into Kai's bedroom showed it was empty. But the door to the hallway was open.

I was opening Unity so I could work on the game I was designing for Video Game Production Class when I heard a loud, angry voice.

"How stupid are you?"

I instinctively ducked.

The voice was coming from Kai's house.

"Dad, please, I didn't mean—"

Kai's voice was drowned out by his dad's, who was off on another tirade. He used some choice four letter words between adjectives that included "idiotic," "selfish," "dumb," and "braindead."

I sat frozen at my desk, reeling. Whose parents talked to them that way?

And how had I never realized that Kai's dad was such a jerk? Anytime I'd seen him outside his house, he'd been prim, proper and smiling. A gentleman.

But the way he was currently speaking to his son curdled my stomach. How humiliating. I suddenly felt terrible for eavesdropping. Like I'd stumbled into a deeply personal moment that nobody was meant to witness. Kai may have been a jerk, but I was sure he had feelings.

I put my headphones back on, opened Spotify, and loaded my "Game Design" playlist, letting the electric guitar riffs of my favorite band, The Luminous, drown out the Taylor family domestic drama. It was none of my business, anyway.

Soon, I was lost in my project, Kai completely forgotten.

Today, I was continuing to build a version of Breakout – an old-school arcade game. It was kind of like Pong – you controlled a paddle, and a ball bounced off your paddle and smashed into some blocks, destroying them. Each time the ball bounced off the blocks, it sped up. I was trying to create a special block that, when you hit it, would create a second ball that you had to worry about.

The last light of the afternoon faded into the wintery darkness of nightfall. I was so wrapped up in coding, music blaring through my headphones as time slipped away, irrelevant, that I missed the first few knocks on the window.

It was during a lull between songs that a *tap-tap-tap* propelled me back to reality.

What the heck?

I ran over to my window… and was greeted by the sight of Kai, backlit by his bedroom light, leaning out of his window. He was holding a crooked metal rod, which looked like a series of coat hangers that had been twisted together.

The tip of the rod scratched my window.

Weird way to get my attention, but… innovative.

I threw open my window. The icy January wind whistled around my head and I shivered.

"Fi-na-llyyy," Kai said. "What took you so long? My hands are almost numb."

Any misplaced trace of sympathy I'd had for my neighbor dried up like a puddle in the desert. "What are you doing to my window?"

"Giving it a gentle caress." Kai pulled the rod back inside and threw it on his floor. He smiled at me. "It's your lucky day. I need your help, Mac Attack."

"Good luck with that," I snapped, already preparing to slam my window.

But before I could shut it, Kai's voice came again. Softer, this time. "Please. Wait."

I sighed. "You have three seconds."

"I forgot my VGP textbook at school. Can I borrow yours?"

I rolled my eyes. "Drive back to school and get yours."

"I… can't." A hint of embarrassment colored Kai's words.

I pointed to the front of his house, where his flashy Audi was parked. "Last I checked, you had a vehicle, an able body, and a driver's license."

A flash of a grin danced over Kai's face. "An able body, you say?"

"Three seconds are up, Taylor." I reached up to close my window, done with this crap. I had better things to do than be Mr. All Star's cheap entertainment.

"Wait, wait — sorry, I'm sorry," Kai called. His tone was full of barely disguised laughter. "Usually, girls like it when I flirt."

"And why do you think that is?"

Kai shrugged. "Low standards, probably."

In spite of myself, I laughed. I tried to hold it back, but all that did was turn my laugh into a strange, half-laugh, half-choking sound. I cleared my throat and tried to look as professional as possible. "I've got things to do, Kai. So let's get to it – why can't you just drive back to school?"

He flushed, the color in his cheeks making him look sweeter than usual. More vulnerable. He looked at me carefully for a long moment. "I guess I'm grounded."

"You guess?"

"I guess." His tone was defiant, an attempt to project a don't-care, casual vibe.

I thought of the Click blast, of his dad shouting insults, and I almost felt bad for Kai again.

Almost.

"You saw the blast, I'm guessing," Kai said. "I'm f–struggling in Video Game Production. I rushed out of school, I didn't think to grab my textbook. So, I need to borrow yours. I'll owe you big time."

"You definitely will," I said. "And I know exactly how you can pay me back."

"How's that?"

"By keeping your shirt on when you work out."

Kai laughed. It wasn't the condescending, patronizing laugh I was used to – the one he used after he teased someone. This laugh was genuine. He put his hand on his heart. "Done. You'll never see me shirtless again. Unless you want to."

"I'll never see you shirtless again," I confirmed. "But now, we have a different problem. How do you want me to get the book to you? I'm not going to throw it."

Secretly, I doubted I could throw it with enough accuracy to get it into his window.

"Already thought of that," Kai said. He held up a length of rope and a small laundry basket. The rope was threaded through the handles. He grinned. "We just need to get creative."

4

MAC

reak.

Loser.

Cheater.

The insults followed me down the hallways of Evermore High. Here I was, walking the same corridors I'd frequented for three whole years, but now that I was on Click's radar, people suddenly had a lot to say about my existence.

I preferred being invisible.

I clutched my books to my chest as I walked, my expression set. As much as I wanted to pull the hood of my sweater over my head and run away, I didn't. Instead. I kept my pace slow and deliberate, standing with my head held high. I'd never show weakness, no matter what anybody said.

I knocked on Principal Potter's door.

"Come in!"

I entered the office, nerves fluttering in my chest.

"Right on time," Principal Potter said. He motioned to an empty chair. "Take a seat, Mackayla."

I slid into the plastic chair, a smile painted on my face. If I was nice, I was sure I could convince him to get me out of this ridiculous prom business.

Principal Potter adjusted his glasses. "How can I help?"

"I'd like my nomination for prom queen to be retracted."

"Why?"

I'd been preparing my speech in my head all day. I'd even dressed the part — nothing screamed "this girl's no prom queen" more than a slightly-stained hoodie, plaid kilt, red braids, black eyeliner, and of course, my trusty Doc Martens. "The most obvious reason is that I'm a junior."

"Irregular, but not a reason to retract the nomination."

"Not irregular – unheard of," I said. "I looked it up. No junior has ever been nominated. Last year, Chase Jones was starting quarterback and Hailey Danielson was cheer captain. But, because they were juniors, even *they* didn't get nominated. And they were, like, the most popular people in the school. The seniors take prom court super seriously. It's their thing."

"Yet, not against the rules," Principal Potter replied. "Nowhere in the Evermore rulebook does it stipulate that a member of the junior class cannot be nominated to the prom court. I checked before confirming your nomination. Is there anything else?"

My first approach had failed, but I had another trick up my sleeve.

"I also have stage fright," I said. "Standing up there, in front of people? It makes me want to throw up. What if I throw up in front of everyone?"

Principal Potter's eyes glazed over. "Used to have stage fright myself. When I had to talk to a room full of people, I'd freeze up. But, there's one solution that's sure to work – exposure therapy. You need to fight this head on. If you have stage fright, I can think of no better thing for you than to run for prom queen."

Ugh. I wasn't getting anywhere, which meant I needed to resort to my final argument. It was a two-pronged approach. "Fine. How about the fact that I don't want to be prom queen? And anyone who knows me would know that. Which means – someone set me up."

"Like a prank?" Principal Potter drummed his fingers on the desk. "If it is a prank, it's very elaborate. How do you suppose you secured enough votes?"

I shrugged. "They rigged it, probably."

"The staff were responsible for counting the votes, Mackayla. So, unless you are accusing one of our faculty of setting you up—"

"I'm not," I said quickly.

He nodded. "That's what I thought."

The bell rang, the trill cutting through the uncomfortable atmosphere in the office.

"I guess I'll go to class," I mumbled. I wasn't used to giving up this easily. "There's seriously nothing that can be done? You're sure?"

"Positive," Principal Potter said. "Consider it an honor – many girls would die to be in your spot."

I exhaled, resigned to my life as prom queen nominee. Stupid school. Stupid rules. Why wouldn't he let me get out of this dumb production? Why not give the nomination to someone who actually wants it?

As I left his office, I came to a decision. Principal Potter wouldn't let me give up the nomination, but he couldn't force me to run, either. I wouldn't campaign for votes – I'd leave that to Jordyn and Madison. Let them dazzle while I faded into the background, completely forgotten.

My phone buzzed.

More from Click.

Ever wonder how a JUNIOR was able to get nominated for Prom Queen? We have the answer: a fixed ballot. Apparently, our lovely Mackayla swapped her name with Hailey's so she could get nominated and become more popular. Newsflash, Mackayla: Evermore's never going to vote for some loser junior. Especially not when they cheated.

I stared at my phone screen.

Click was accusing me of faking the ballot? Typical. Why would I do that? This was standard Evermore elitism – assuming that *everyone* wanted to be prom queen or king

And yet again, people were calling me a cheater. But there was something more going on. Like why did Click call itself a "we"? Had it done that before? It must have... but I couldn't shake the feeling that things were getting increasingly personal.

Was there a target on my back? Or was I just cannon fodder for a stupid prank?

5

KAI

*I*t was crunch time.

Tonight, we had an away game against the Eastmount Knights, one of our division rivals. If the universe was on my side, I'd be in my uniform and sinking three-pointers in a few hours.

If the universe wasn't on my side… it would be more of what happened the other night.

After my dad found out I was suspended, he laid into me for hours. He shouted about how I was throwing my future away, how I'd never get to play college ball like he did. I tried to tell him that I wasn't slacking on purpose, but he insisted that I was, because there was no way I was actually dumb enough to fail a "stupid class about video games."

When he was done berating me, I borrowed Mac's textbook and got down to business. I spent the night trying to build a simple pong game, with disastrous results. I couldn't figure out why, but seventy-five percent of the time, when I tried to turn on the game, it didn't start. I'd checked through the code repeatedly and couldn't figure out where I'd made a mistake.

And now, time was up.

Mr. Vargas patrolled the room, chatting with each student as he examined their work. He talked to them about their game, took some notes, and pointed out any issues that he saw.

I waited impatiently, jiggling my leg so hard it smacked my desk. Like the rest of the team, I wore my Evermore Panthers hoodie. It was a game day tradition. I doubted Mr. Vargas would be swayed by athletic apparel, but a guy could hope.

Mr. Vargas reached Mac's desk. She casually flipped open her laptop and turned on her game. It looked like an advanced version of the old arcade game "Breakout." Mac was babbling a mile a minute, and Mr. Vargas bent forward, listening intently.

When it came to video games, no one could touch Mac. It was like she was LeBron and the rest of us had never seen a ball before.

I glanced at my laptop and my nerves bubbled to the surface. How hard could it be to create a working version of Pong? Everyone else had figured it out. The semester had just started and already I was so far behind. Why, oh why, had I been dumb enough to think that this would be an easy computer science credit? Why didn't I just take Intro to MS Office Suite? Everyone else on the team did.

But me? *No, that class sounded too boring.*

I would take boring over failure.

By the time Vargas reached my desk, my palms were sweaty.

"Mr. Taylor. Did you get it working properly?"

"Yep," I said with way more confidence than I felt.

"Let's see."

I pressed play.

The title screen flashed – and then disappeared, replaced by an error code. The program had crashed.

My heart hit the linoleum.

Vargas gestured to my sweatshirt. "Maybe the attire was a little premature, Mr. Taylor. You won't be playing tonight."

"Guess not," I said, defeated.

The other students weren't staring, not outright, but they were listening. And immediately after Vargas announced that I wouldn't be playing in the game tonight, they started texting. Were they telling their friends or putting out a Click blast?

It didn't matter.

My cheeks burned. I'd failed. Again.

I'd let my team down. Again.

I'd let my dad down. Again.

Maybe Click was right. Maybe I was stupid.

"Check the code in your title screen segment. The problem should be in there," Mr. Vargas said. He continued to the next desk.

I pretended to busy myself with my laptop. Everyone would eventually stop staring if I just acted casual. I was glad none of my friends were in this class. Although that wouldn't do me much good for long – there was a Click blast incoming, I was sure of it.

When the bell finally rang, I made my way to Mackayla's desk.

"Thanks for the book," I said, setting the textbook on her desk. "Guess I missed a step."

"Guess so," she said. "You okay?"

She sounded… concerned. Though I had no idea why – it wasn't like we had a history of being nice to each other. If anything, she should've been doing cartwheels after seeing me fail again.

I could take a lot.

But the hint of pity in her voice?

That, I couldn't take.

"I just wanted to see if the team could win without me tonight," I lied. I looked at my fingernails to feign nonchalance. "Bet they can't."

The concern in Mac's expression was quickly replaced by contempt, like I'd hoped. She rolled her eyes and threw up her hands, exasperated. "If your confidence was electricity, you could power all of Evermore."

"Are you trying to tell me I light up your life, Mac & Cheese?" I asked with an innocent smile.

Mac rolled her eyes and stood. "Enjoy the game. Try not to get splinters from the bench."

Before I could respond, she stormed off.

I held the grin on my face, though I didn't much feel like smiling.

Enjoy the bench. That hurt.

And I'd completely deserved it.

But scorn was better than pity.

6

KAI

$\mathcal{I}$ sat on the bench and watched my team lose. After our first loss of the season, the rest of my week only got worse. My teammates weren't exactly understanding about me missing the game. Star athletes weren't supposed to get benched. With every snide joke they made, there was an implication – get back on the court as soon as possible, or else.

But, I wasn't making much progress in that department. I was trying in Video Game Production, but the class was still kicking my butt. I spent hours every night trying to work my way through lines of code, but every time I fixed one bug, I created two more.

Come Friday afternoon, I was sitting at the back of the class, listening to Mr. Vargas explain how certain video game franchises used lore and flavor text as a form of storytelling. Then, he talked about branching decision trees based on user input.

He may as well have been speaking Japanese.

The bell rang and class ended.

My week was over.

Finally.

"Mr. Taylor and Miss Lafelle, could you please stay a minute?" Mr. Vargas asked as the rest of the class filtered out.

I glanced at Mackayla, who looked as confused as I felt. Her red hair was pulled back in a severe ponytail, and it made her heavily-mascaraed eyes look huge. She caught me looking at her, crossed her eyes, and stuck out her tongue.

I bit back a laugh.

After the rest of the students had left, Mr. Vargas shut the door. "I imagine you're wondering why I kept you back?"

"I assume I'm in trouble," I said. "No idea what Little Mac did."

"Bonus points for the reference, Taylor. You used my name *and* it was from a video game," Mac said.

"At least I'm improving at something," I muttered.

"And that's what I would like to talk to you both about," Mr. Vargas said. He tapped the tips of his index fingers together, choosing his next words carefully. "I think that you both could benefit from what I'm about to suggest."

I sat a little straighter. I would do almost anything to get back on the court.

"Mackayla, you are a natural coder. Leagues ahead of anyone else in this class. You're practically a professional already, and I believe the content of this curriculum is not entirely stimulating to your abilities." Mr. Vargas turned his focus to me. "And it's no secret that you're struggling, Mr. Taylor. Your coach has made me well aware of how much it's affecting the team. I'm not going to give you an easy grade, but I'm willing to work with you. Which is why I would like to suggest that we come to a tutoring agreement between the two of you."

Before I could process what Mr. Vargas said, Mackayla was babbling.

"What? Why do I get punished? If Kai wants to get back

on the team, he should do it himself." Blood bloomed under her pale cheeks as she spoke. "I am NOT doing his work for him. This is just another example—"

Mr. Vargas held up his hands, and, remarkably, Mackayla went silent. The teacher cleared his throat. "You will not be doing any work for him – you'd simply be lending a second set of eyes. I know how badly you want to work in the industry. Proof that you're able to work with others, that you're able to work on a team, will take you a long way. As will a personal recommendation from someone who's worked in the industry before... perhaps prior to their teaching career."

Mackayla pressed her lips together as she mulled over his words. It was rumored that Mr. Vargas had worked at an AAA studio before coming to Evermore, but it had never been confirmed.

With Mac now quiet, I had my own objections. Namely, I didn't want to risk Mackayla learning how dumb I really was.

"What if I don't want a tutor?"

Mr. Vargas stared at me. "You should reframe your question, Mr. Taylor. What do you want more? To fail this class without help and not play basketball again this season, or to pass this class and have the opportunity to lead your team to victory?"

Well, when he put it like that...

"That's what I thought." Mr. Vargas nodded in approval, before reaching into his desk drawer. He retrieved two small slips of paper and passed them to Mac. "Now I'm not calling this a bribe in any way, shape, or form — but I thought this could sweeten the deal for you, Mackayla. Get Kai's grade up, and these are yours."

Mac's eyes were saucers as she stared at the papers in her hands. I moved closer so I could see.

They were tickets. To a video game conference in Denver.

Mac was looking at them like she'd won courtside seats to Game 7 of the NBA finals.

She ran her finger over the edge of the tickets, then turned to me. "You will get your grades up."

"You make it sound like a threat."

"It is a threat," Mackayla said. She winked, then looked back to Mr. Vargas. "I'm down."

I hesitated. "If I do this, can I play again right away?"

Mr. Vargas shook his head. "You can play again when your grades improve."

"Good," Mac said. "If you can't play until your grades go up, I know that you'll take this seriously."

Why would she just assume I wouldn't take this seriously? I glared at her. "You better be as good at coding as you think you are."

"I'm better, actually," Mac said.

"Perhaps this will be a growing experience for you both," Mr. Vargas said. His mouth was twitching like he was trying not to laugh. "I'm rooting for both of you to succeed. I don't want you to think otherwise."

His expression was sincere, but I still couldn't quite believe him.

7

MAC

*W*hat had I just agreed to?

I stood in shock, the realization hitting me – I agreed to tutor Kai Taylor, the cocky jerk who embodied everything I hated about Evermore.

What was WRONG with me?

Mr. Vargas had seen my kryptonite, and exploited it to his advantage. GameON Video Game Expo was literally impossible to get tickets to — believe me, I had tried.

Tutoring Kai would be worth it. For this, it would.

Kai was standing near the window, looking out at the snow. He hadn't moved since Mr. Vargas left the room. I wondered if the same realization was hitting him, too.

"What's with the statue act?" I asked.

His dark eyes snapped left, locking on mine. For a moment, there was sadness. But the emotion was gone as quickly as it had arrived. He looked back out the window. "This blizzard's supposed to be rough."

"Then I better get home before I'm forced to trudge through three feet of snow." I shivered. The thought of walking a mile home was enough to ruin what was left of my good mood.

"You don't drive?"

"I can drive. I just don't have a car."

"Oh," he continued without looking away from the window. "Need a ride?"

"Excuse me?"

"Need. A. Ride. Home?" He leaned against the window, the kind of casual pose a model might have in a fashion catalog. And Kai was definitely hot enough to be a model.

Which was annoying.

But, it totally didn't influence my decision to accept a ride.

I nodded, and Kai smiled cheekily. "Come on then, Macadamia Nut. Let's get you home."

A FEW MINUTES LATER, I was sitting in the passenger seat of Kai Taylor's Audi. His car was surprisingly neat and tidy.

"It's actually clean," I said. Not the best conversational icebreaker I've ever had. "So your dad grounds you and still lets you take the car?"

Kai snorted. "Not like *he* was going to drive me to school."

He leaned over and turned the volume up on the stereo. The sounds of my favorite song by The Luminous filled the vehicle.

My eyebrows shot into my hairline. "You like The Luminous?"

He took his eyes off the road for a moment, a half-smile playing on his lips as he looked at me. "Doesn't everybody?"

"Didn't think jocks had good taste in music." I tried my best to sound haughty, but there was no venom in my tone.

"You sure have a lot of big opinions for a person being saved from snowmageddon."

I smiled sheepishly. Looked down at my hands. "Sorry. Thank you for the ride."

"We'll call it even for letting me borrow your book."

"Deal."

Kai Taylor liking The Luminous surprised me. But what really surprised me was when he cranked the volume, turned his steering wheel into a drum, and started singing along. I didn't say a word – I just stared at him while he belted out lyrics until his voice went hoarse.

And what surprised me even more was that I started singing as well. Not as loud as Kai – I wasn't that bold – but loud enough that he could hear me.

Was I… were we… having fun? We liked the same music and we both had terrible voices. Bantering back and forth? That was fun, too. A prickly sensation erupted on my skin. Kai Taylor was meant to be my mortal enemy. But here he was, giving me a ride home and singing along to one of my favorite songs. It was upsetting my equilibrium.

We were silent for the next few blocks. By the time Kai pulled into his driveway, I couldn't wait to get out of the car and away from this strange feeling building in me.

Both of our phones vibrated at once.

That could only mean one thing –

A Click blast.

Kai turned off the ignition. He ran his hands through his hair, messing it up. Then he picked up his phone carefully, like it was a loaded gun. "Think it's about you or me this time?"

"It's been a few hours since they mentioned me," I said. I laughed derisively to show I didn't care. But my heartbeat quickened as I swiped my phone open.

I was correct — this time, the target was on my back.

Click had posted the most unflattering picture of me I'd ever seen. I was standing by my locker, wearing my gym clothes and a messy ponytail. My arm was raised, and I was sniffing my armpit. The caption beneath the photo?

Something smells fishy about one of the candidates for Prom Queen.

I wanted to die.

Kai looked at me solemnly. "If it's any consolation, I don't think you smell like fish."

"I was on my way to gym class!" I shrieked. "I was trying to remember if I'd put deodorant on."

"Sorry, sorry." Kai held up his hands, his expression sobering. He actually looked remorseful. "I shouldn't laugh. I know how much this sucks. You okay?"

I rocked backwards, knocking my head against the car seat headrest. "I'm just so sick of this bullying. I didn't ask for or want any of this. Someone set me up. And now, just because I'm a prom queen candidate who doesn't wave pom poms at football games or wear a push-up bra, everyone seems to think I'm fair game."

I knew I was ranting, but I didn't care. The entire week of beratement, name calling, and public humiliation was suffocating me. "The only reason Click has so much power is because everyone gives it so much power. And Click does the worst kind of bullying — it allows everybody to anonymously weigh in with their opinions at the cost of somebody else's feelings. I just wish there was a world where I could take Click on. Win this stupid prom queen thing just to show them all that bullying doesn't always win."

Kai drummed his fingers on the steering wheel, then nodded. "You've got my vote."

Another surprise from Kai Taylor. "Your vote?"

"I'm saying I agree. Click is the worst. And you're not its first victim. It has made so many people suffer. Last week,

Click loved me. This week, I'm the worst person in the world."

"Besides me," I said. I'd forgotten how Click had come after Kai for being dumb. Being popular, in the Evermore spotlight, meant one thing: the further you rose, the further you'd fall. Click had come for Chase Jones, Hailey Danielson, and Jordyn Jones. In the fall, it had hunted Noah Lyons. And now, it was after me.

"I just wish we could get rid of it," I said. "Or that I win this stupid prom queen thing so everyone can realize it doesn't have any power."

Kai narrowed his eyes. "You could, you know."

"Could what?"

"Take a real run at prom queen. Prove the haters wrong."

I laughed sharply. "And how do you propose I do that?"

"I could help."

"You'd help me?" My voice cracked. I cleared my throat and tried again. "You'd help me?"

Kai smiled. Not an arrogant smirk or a cocky grin, but a real, honest smile. "I know you don't want to tutor me, but the fact is, I really need the help. Basketball is everything to me, I can't get kicked off the team. Plus, I also hate Click. The jerks behind it deserve to be proved wrong."

The idea seemed crazy.

Impossible.

But, was it?

Taking down Click. It would do so much good for Evermore High. Save future students so much pain. Future students like Shaun.

My heart ached as I imagined my little brother as a freshman at Evermore High. Would Click broadcast every social cue he missed?

I couldn't let that happen.

"How would we even do that?" I asked. Despite my best efforts, a small ray of hope was sparking in my chest.

"Simple. I'll manage your campaign. Throw my support behind you. Being a star athlete has status, right? We can ask everyone who's ever felt victimized by Click to stand behind you."

"This is so insane, it might almost work."

"I can see it now: Mackayla Lafelle, the Anti Prom Queen."

"The Anti Prom Queen," I repeated. A smile tugged at my lips.

"What do you think? You really commit to helping me get my grades up, and I'll really commit to helping you win this thing. We can take down Click together."

Could we actually pull this off?

"Think about all the people you'd be helping," Kai said.

"We'd be helping," I corrected.

We could do this.

We *would* do this.

For everyone who'd ever been bullied, victimized, made to feel shame or embarrassment for being different or for not fitting in. I'd put myself out there, campaign for change that needed to happen.

I exhaled, a rush of adrenaline shooting through my veins. "I'm in. Tell me what to do, and I'll do it."

Kai chewed his lower lip. Then, he stuck his hand out. "Deal?"

I shook it. "Deal."

Our hands stayed connected a moment too long, and to my surprise, a jolt of electricity crackled through me. I quickly jerked my hand out of his, and averted my gaze. If he was laughing at me, I didn't want to see it.

"I'd better get home, thanks for the ride."

Kai nodded. "Anytime."

I was halfway down the driveway when he called. "Oh, and Macbeth?"

I spun around, then silently cursed myself for responding to yet another one of his stupid nicknames. I placed my hands on my hips. "Yes?"

"Try not to get caught smelling yourself again."

8

MAC

*N*ormally, there wasn't anything I couldn't cure with a donut. When I was sad, nervous, or stressed, a sugary pick-me-up was the perfect way to take the edge off. I could go with an old-fashioned covered with sparkling sugar, a honey-glazed cruller, or a chocolate dip.

But today, I wasn't hungry.

"Aren't you going to eat that?" Sofia sat across the table from me, eyeing my untouched donuts – a Boston crème and a caramel apple fritter.

I shook my head and pushed the plate towards her.

Sof swiped the Boston crème and took a massive bite before I had time to change my mind. A blotch of custard fell to her chin and she quickly wiped it away with a napkin.

I laughed. It was Sunday morning, and the two of us were catching up over breakfast – which meant copious amounts of carbs and sugar from our new favorite bakery on Main Street, Love You Forevermore. It was a cute, cozy space, filled with brightly-colored overstuffed armchairs, squashy sofas, shelves of board games and books, and the smell of caramelized sugar.

"So. Prom craziness getting to you yet?" Sofia asked, dabbing at the corner of her mouth with a napkin. Her eyes were soft and full of concern.

I took a sip of my coffee, then grit my teeth. "It's been a weird, weird week."

"Do you know how it happened yet?" Sofia asked, keeping her voice low. The bakery wasn't busy, but Click had eyes everywhere. "Like who nominated you?"

I loved that Sofia cared about me enough to get right down to business. There was no use in pretending that my nomination might've been legitimate.

I took another sip of my coffee. "It was obviously a set up. I mean, everybody knows Hailey was the favorite for queen. It's more than a little suspicious that she wasn't even nominated. Maybe someone's out to get her."

"I don't really think she cared," Sofia said. Her older brother, Dylan, was a prom king nominee himself, so Sofia was well-connected to Evermore's cool crowd. "And Jordyn was more annoyed than excited. She's dreading having to spend time with Madison."

"Those two don't like each other, huh?"

"Madison is Chase's ex-girlfriend. Jordyn's playing her role as the vengeful twin sister." Sofia shrugged. "Though I don't think Jordyn would like Madison anyway."

"I forgot that those two used to date," I said. Back when I was a freshman, Madison and Chase were the Evermore "It" couple. Or, as Sofia jokingly called them, "Chadison."

"Right?" Sofia licked a glob of chocolate frosting off her pinky. "Chase and Abby seem so perfect for each other, it's like they were always together."

"Abby's a saint," I said, sincerely. "I wish I didn't have to go up against Madison."

Sofia's mouth dropped open. "Wait. Are you actually planning to campaign?"

I spread my hands wide on the table and looked Sofia in the eye. "I have a plan."

Sofia, used to my schemes, flipped her eyes skyward. "Sounds ominous. What do you mean, a plan?"

"I'm going to campaign to be Evermore's Anti Prom Queen. You know — revolution, power to the people, taking back our school. I'm going to prove Click wrong, take down that stupid gossip app once and for all. If I can prove that Click isn't as powerful as everyone thinks it is, then people might stop taking it so seriously. And who knows, maybe Click itself will die off."

Sofia screwed up her eyes. Rubbed her face. When she leveled her gaze back at me, she looked tired. "Mac, are you sure about that? It could be reputation suicide."

"Better my head on the chopping block than someone else's," I said, trying my best to sound confident. "I'll take one for the team. Yeah, maybe it's a long shot, but it's worth that shot. You miss 100% of the shots you don't take, you know."

"Powerful," Sofia deadpanned. "You should put that in your prom queen speech."

"Maybe I will." I pulled the plate of donuts back towards myself and bit down on the fritter. All this talk of taking down Click was giving me my appetite back.

Sofia stretched back in her armchair, running her fingers idly over the velvety purple fabric. "If you do this, how are you going to get people to listen to you?"

My mouthful of donut suddenly became difficult to swallow.

"Kaitaylorshelpingme," I mumbled, my rushed words all blending into one.

Sofia took a smug sip of her hot chocolate, her shrewd eyes glimmering knowingly. "Sorry, what was that? I couldn't quite hear you."

"I said, Kaitaylorshelpingme," I repeated, just as fast.

Sofia tilted her head. "Still didn't catch that. Who's helping you?"

"KAI TAYLOR'S HELPING ME!" I yelled. Heads around the bakery turned. I clamped a hand over my mouth, mortified.

Meanwhile, Sofia was practically on the floor. Tears of laughter streamed down her cheeks. "I'm sorry, did you just say that Hot Neighbor Boy, aka your least favorite person in the world, is helping you become prom queen?"

It took me ages to calm her down. Ages. The girl was practically hysterical.

Finally, about a hundred years later, she stopped laughing. But she still had a huge smirk. "I told you that you only hated him because, underneath it all, you really liked him."

I shook my head. "It's not like that. I don't like him. In fact, I still hate him. Big time. Just… not as much as I thought."

My so-called best friend raised her eyebrows. "Sureeeeeee."

"It's the truth! We might be working together now, but outside of this, we're still polar opposites. I'm a dork. He's a jock. An arrogant one at that. Our worlds are totally different — and his world sucks."

"Methinks the lady doth protest too much."

I threw the rest of my donut at her.

9

KAI

*A*nother game, another evening spent warming the bench.

Tonight's opponent? The River Valley High Warriors. We were feeling good, and an infectious enthusiasm ran through us as we got ready in the locker room. Guys were bouncing basketballs off the wall, cheering and shouting and high-fiving. Coach was walking around with his chest puffed out, muttering to himself.

The Warriors, in a word, sucked. Their team was brutal. With or without me playing, Evermore would destroy them. It was nice to have a sure win on the horizon, but it didn't make it any easier for me to be a spectator.

It had only been a week, but I was aching to play the sport I loved again. To make up for missing so much practice, I'd begun dedicating an hour each evening to shooting hoops in my front driveway before going for a 10-mile run — through blizzarding snow, frost, and arctic winds. I was determined to be in tip-top shape upon my return to playing.

Which, with Mac's help, would hopefully be sooner rather than later.

Zane stood on a bench, holding his bottle of Gatorade high. "To dominating the Warriors!"

"To dominating the Warriors!" the team yelled, whooping and hollering.

A chorus of "Panthers! Panthers!" echoed around the locker room. I tried my best to look pumped as I joined in the chant. But, I felt a bit ridiculous. Right now, I was more of a hindrance than a help to my own team.

It was a feeling I wasn't used to.

And it wasn't a good feeling.

At all.

After everyone went back to changing, Zane jumped off the bench, landing deftly next to me. He took a seat and started lacing his shoes. "How you holding up, Taylor?"

I shrugged. Kicked my foot against the bench leg. "Wish I could play. They keep me out of the game and you might even catch me for the scoring lead."

Zane laughed. "Not unless they keep you out for the entire season. Any chance Vargas might lift your suspension? Coach seemed pretty pissed about the whole thing."

I shook my head. "He's pretty intense — he's not going to let me play again until my grades improve."

What I didn't tell Zane was that my dad had called the school to complain. Then, he'd had me write an apology letter to Mr. Vargas. Coach McMorris had even petitioned the principal. But Mr. Vargas hadn't budged — the rules were the rules, he said. Nothing could be done.

"Figure it out, man," Zane said. "We need you back for playoffs."

"Working on it. Even got myself a tutor."

Zane squinted at me, skeptical. "What? Who?"

"Mackayla Lafelle."

Zane laughed. "The weird girl?"

I bristled. For some reason, it bothered me to hear him

call her weird. I felt like I had to explain myself. "She's the best in the class, dude. And she's my neighbor, so that's convenient."

"Best in the class or not, she's still weird." Zane's lip curled in distaste. "You see that pic of her smelling herself?"

"Like you've never checked to see if you're wearing deodorant," I said.

"She still watch you workout?" Zane pulled his Panthers jersey over his head. The silver outline of the big cat emblem glimmered under the harsh lights of the locker room. "I bet that chick's into you. Got some weird, witchy-girl crush. She probably has a voodoo doll made out of your hair."

Zane snickered at his lame joke, then blinked in surprise when he saw I wasn't joining in.

"She's not into me," I insisted, barely keeping my temper in check. "She's just doing me a favor, helping get my grades up."

"Relax, man. I'm joking." He clapped me on my back so hard I almost choked. "Come on, Taylor. You're acting like you're into her, too. She slip you a love potion or something?"

I let out a weak laugh. "There is absolutely nothing going on between me and Mackayla Lafelle. She's not into me. And I am definitely not into her. Period."

Zane gave me an exaggerated wink. "Whatever you say."

I didn't get a chance to argue. Coach blew his whistle, rounding everybody up.

It was time.

Heads held high, the team walked out of the locker room and onto the court to a roar of applause. They held their hands in the air, soaking in the support. Lights flashed. The school fight song played. The cheerleaders waved their pom poms and turned backflips.

I trailed behind, and when I got out on the court, I slipped onto the bench as quietly as possible.

Suddenly, I felt very alone.

MAC

I did not like Kai Taylor.
     I did not like Kai Taylor.
I did not like Kai Taylor.

The thought was scrawled into my mind repeatedly as I took my seat in Video Game Production and unpacked my laptop. Sofia claimed that thinking about someone when they weren't around was a sign you liked them; she also said that love and hate were two sides of the same coin. Whatever that was supposed to mean. She could think what she wanted, but I knew the truth.

I did not like Kai Taylor.

"This seat taken, Macklemore?" Kai stood by the chair next to me, running his finger along the sleeve of my vintage, crushed peacoat. Without waiting for a response, he moved the coat out of the way and slid into the empty chair.

"What if it was taken?" I asked.

"It wasn't. And if anyone was sitting here, I'd just kick them trout."

I groaned. Ever since Click had accused me of smelling like fish, Kai had taken to dropping in fish puns whenever possible. It amazed me that someone who loved puns so much was still considered popular.

Kai pulled out his laptop. "If you're tutoring me, we may as well sit together. Maybe I can learn through osmosis. Just absorb all that coding knowledge."

I eyed Kai warily. The weird kid and the jock, sitting together. Frankly, I was surprised Click hadn't already lit us up. I looked around to make sure no one was watching. "Aren't people going to talk?"

"Probably," Kai said. "But, if you want to be prom queen, you need people to talk about you. And what better way to get them to talk than for me to grace you with my presence?"

"You don't think people will find it a bit fishy?"

Kai snorted – like actually snorted – with laughter.

I had to bite my cheek to keep from grinning too hard. The snort was so ridiculous, so uncool, that for a split second, the chic jock veneer cracked and showed an adorably geeky boy underneath.

Kai's dark eyes glittered. They looked even darker today, thanks to the form-fitting black long sleeve shirt he was wearing. Which, by the way, looked amazing on him – it accentuated his tall, fit frame.

Not that I'd noticed.

Heat rose to my cheeks. To distract myself – and Kai, if necessary – I opened the tutoring plan I'd made. "This is what we're going to be working on," I said. "You'll need to start by making Pong. Then we'll move you to a platformer, like Mario, a text RPG, and a very simple sports game. I know a lot of last semester's class used fencing because it was easier to program – basically rock paper scissors, but with graphics."

Kai pulled his chair closer, and the woodsy, warm scent of his cologne filled the air. He raked his hands through his hair and sighed. "That's... a lot."

"Part of the class," I said. "Don't worry about it – you can do it."

"You think I can?" Kai sounded uncertain. "This comes naturally to you, but not to me. I may as well be taking Latin."

"I have every bit of confidence in you," I said, smiling my best teacher smile. Confidence was important when you were learning. "And that was the deal, right? I teach you how to code video games, you turn me into a queen."

"An Anti-Queen."

"Much better," I said. "No one's about to confuse me with royalty. Now, let's get started."

CLASS PASSED QUICKLY. Mr. Vargas touched on some more advanced concepts, including the hilariously-named "Coyote Time" concept, before regaling us with a few tales from his own experience in the industry.

Next to me, Kai looked like he'd just sat through a lecture in a foreign language. The bell rung, and he slumped in his seat with a loud sigh. "I don't know how you're able to understand any of this."

"Just takes time. And for you to stay awake." I'd been watching Kai through most of the class. I'd caught him nodding off at least once – which didn't bode well for my chances of winning tickets to the expo.

"I tried to listen," Kai said, stifling another yawn. "But after five minutes, I was so lost there was no point."

"I'll text you to confirm our study session tomorrow." I clambered to my feet, trying my best to act like it was completely normal that I had Kai Taylor's phone number. And that he had mine. The latter was the bigger concern – what if he started sending me stupid Mac-related GIFs at three in the morning? He was annoying enough even without 24-hour access to torture me.

Kai stood. "You hungry? I'm hungry. We should eat."

"What?" I was so caught off guard by what he said that I nearly dropped my laptop. "Like, together?"

"Yeah."

"But... why?" It was one thing to sit next to Kai in a class of twenty-five kids. It was something else entirely to eat lunch with him in the cafeteria, where anyone could see us. I could already feel the stares and hear the whispers. "Is this about prom queen?"

"What else?" Kai slung his laptop bag over his shoulder. "We need to go over your plan anyway. And if you're seen with me, that'll kickstart the rumor mill. Which is what you need. You're not exactly Ms. Popular."

I watched as the rest of the students filtered out of class. Like it or not, Kai had a point. The more I was seen with him, the more Click would notice. And if I wanted to win prom queen, I needed to be in Click's crosshairs – especially if I was rebelling against the stupid app. Plus, there was a small part of me that didn't mind the thought of eating lunch with Kai. Which was weird.

Extremely weird.

I glanced out the window, checking for flying pigs, before giving Kai his response. "Fine. Let's do this."

We stepped out into the quad, and I wrapped my coat around me, protecting myself from the cold winter wind. My short legs struggled to keep up with Kai's long strides.

We reached the cafeteria.

Kai pushed the door open, and I immediately moved behind him, effectively making him my human shield. It didn't work – he dodged out of the way and slung his arm around my shoulder.

"Be more obvious, Taylor," I muttered sarcastically.

"Best defense is a good offense," Kai said. He handed me a tray.

Not that I needed one – I'd lost my appetite while drowning in the sea of stares. Still, I dutifully grabbed a tuna sandwich, a bag of chips, and an over-sized chocolate chip cookie. Kai filled his tray with a plate of fries, three chicken burgers, two chocolate milks, and a half-dozen jumbo cookies.

My eyes bulged. "Are we eating with other people, or are you just really hungry?"

"Not that hungry," Kai said. "Why?"

"No reason."

We found an empty table in the corner. Kai either didn't notice that everyone was staring, or he didn't care. I supposed that, when you became as popular as he was, you got used to the looks. By the time I'd sat and unwrapped my tuna sandwich, Kai had already polished off his first chicken burger and downed a chocolate milk.

"So, are you ready for it?" he asked.

"Ready for…?"

"To learn how to become Evermore's next prom queen."

My appetite, which had returned at the smell of food, quickly retreated again at the thought of willingly putting myself in the spotlight. I poked my tuna sandwich. It was mushy. "I guess."

"Good. To become prom queen, you're gonna need to do four things. Number one, you'll need to start attending social gatherings. Parties, events, and all that. Try to mingle, have fun, and try to look like you didn't come just to butcher the popular kids with an ax."

"But what if—"

"Number two," Kai said, ignoring my protests. "Campaign Day. We'll need to do something that will help you stand out."

"Shouldn't be hard," I said.

Kai dipped a French fry in ketchup and popped it in his mouth. "Number three – you need to get involved in the school. People need to see your face, and they need to see that you care about making Evermore a better place."

"But Madison—"

"Madison is a cheerleader who smiles for pep rallies, participates in charity events, and sweet talks everyone."

"But she doesn't even mean it."

"Doesn't have to mean it," Kai said. "The important part is that she shows up. Which means you have to show up, too. And since you do plan to make Evermore a better place, this should be even easier for you."

"As long as you don't make me dress up like a Barbie."

"Why would you think that?" Kai looked genuinely surprised. "You have a really cool style. It's unique. Don't worry about it – just own who you are."

I studied his face, waiting to see his mouth twitching. Waiting for a grin or smirk to appear. For the punchline.

But his expression was serious.

He meant it.

Receiving an unexpected compliment from Kai sent a rush of heat through my body.

Kai didn't notice – he was too involved with his chocolate milk. "And, last, we have the prom parade. Everyone's supposed to create a themed float to get people talking."

Ah, yes. Evermore High's famous prom parade. The potential kings and queens hopped on their floats and paraded down the center of Main Street. It was the closest thing Main Street allowed to a vehicle. I forced myself to take a bite of my tuna sandwich. "Is that it, then?"

"Just one more thing."

"But you said four?"

Kai shrugged. "Things change."

"What is it?"

"You need to send a message to the school. Tell them — tell Click — that you're a real player, that you're in this thing to win. Show Evermore that you're not a joke."

I stared at Kai. "You want me to *voluntarily* put myself in a Click blast? Is that why you wanted me to come to the cafeteria?"

"That and the food," Kai said. "This is where all the best Evermore scandals unfold. And this time, you want people to pay attention."

I glanced around the cafeteria. People were looking at us, whispering. Judging.

Kai was right. I had to step up to the challenge, publicly. It was the only way to let Click know I was standing up for myself.

"How should I—"

"Give me your phone," Kai said.

I passed him my phone. He angled it at my face and started recording.

Suddenly, I felt very nervous. Once I sent out the blast, there was truly no going back.

Kai's eyes met mine. "You can do this, Mac."

"No pun?"

"Not this time."

I took a deep breath, cleared my throat, and looked directly into the camera. "Hi, Evermore. You all know me as that weird girl who got nominated for prom queen. I don't know how it happened, and honestly, I wasn't going to campaign. But then, Click had to get involved. So now I *am* going to run. But I'm not running as your prom queen. I'm running as the Anti Prom Queen. I'm running for everyone who's ever felt victimized or humiliated by Click. And, at the end of all this, I'm going to take Click down. That's a promise."

When I finished speaking, I took another deep breath. I was surprised by how angry I felt. It had all come bubbling out as I talked.

Kai looked up from my phone, his face full of... admiration?

"We should send this," Kai said. "Before you overthink it."

I nodded. "Do it."

Kai sent the Click blast, and a few seconds later, every phone in the cafeteria started to vibrate.

If people were looking before, they were flat-out staring now.

But the freakiest part of all?

No one said a word. Everyone looked at me in complete silence. Were they happy? Proud? Annoyed? Exasperated? It was impossible to tell.

Before I could say anything, the phones started buzzing again.

My phone vibrated in Kai's hand.

He raised his eyebrows. "It's from Click."

I took my phone and opened the message.

Click never says no to a challenge. Game on, Evermore. May the best person win. #MacvsClick

11

MAC

I stood in front of my mirror and checked my teeth. Mom had served spinach salad at dinner, and now, I was paranoid that, when Kai came over, he'd spot little bits of green in my smile. Your appearance could be flawless, but if you had spinach in your teeth, it was game over.

"I thought you didn't care what he thought about you?" Sofia's voice came from my phone, which was propped up on my desk.

"I don't," I said. I used a toothpick to remove the last piece of spinach. Better. "It's not about Kai. I don't want *anyone* to see me with spinach in my teeth."

"Suuuuuuurrrrre."

"Use more sarcasm, Sof."

Thwap.

Something was stuck to my window.

I snapped up my phone. "Gotta go."

"Say hi to your lov—"

I ended the call before Sofia finished, then checked my window.

A foam dart stuck to the glass.

I opened the window and the dart fell to the ground, landing on the lawn beside two other darts.

"It's harder to aim than you think," Kai said, spinning the dart gun around his finger like he was a sheriff in the old west.

"I can see that," I said, still looking at the darts on my lawn. My heart did a small flip as I looked up at Kai. He was wearing a plain t-shirt and jeans, but they both fit him perfectly. But when you were that athletic, everything fit you perfectly. I crossed my arms. "Aren't you supposed to be at my front door about now?"

Kai smiled sadly. "Phone got confiscated. And Dad says I'm not allowed to leave the house."

"Not even for tutoring?"

"I tried to tell him, but he thought I was lying." Kai shrugged. "Not that I can blame him. Call it a bad habit."

"I see." I glanced at my desk, which had two chairs set up in front of my computer. All of the programs we were going to use were open, just waiting for us to start typing in code. "I don't know how we're going to do this if you can't come over."

"Teach me through the window?"

I laughed. "It's not that easy."

"There's got to be something," Kai said. He must have really wanted to get back on the basketball team. "Anything?"

"I think I can help," I said. And, before I could think too much about it, I was on my feet.

A moment later, I was standing on the Taylors' doorstep, ready to knock.

I almost chickened out.

Almost.

And when Mr. Taylor answered, bits of soup still stuck in his graying beard, I wished I had.

"You're the girl next door," he said.

"That's me," I replied. For some reason, I gave a slight bow, like I was speaking to royalty. If Kai's dad thought this was weird, he was too polite to say so. Though his eyebrows did shoot up so far they were now hovering above his head. I peered past him, trying my best to look confused. "Where's Kai? I'm supposed to be tutoring him for one of our classes."

Mr. Taylor scoffed. "My son got a tutor? I doubt it. How much is he paying you?"

"About nothing," I said. A wave of annoyance brushed against me. I crossed my arms. "Kai's late. If I'm going to get his marks up, I'll need you to make sure he's on time in the future. He has a lot of ground to make up."

"He's putting you up to this."

I pressed my lips together into a cold, steely look. "Mr. Taylor. I can assure you, I would rather not spend my evening tutoring your son. But, I told Mr. Vargas I would. So I will. Unless you would like me to tell him – and the principal, I might add – that I was unable to assist in Kai's education because his father stopped me."

Mr. Taylor frowned.

I sighed, shrugged, then started to walk back to my house. "If that's the way you want it…"

"So, this is what the end result will look like."

I clicked a button and a simplified version of Pong came to life. There were two white paddles – one that you could move with the arrow keys – and a white ball bouncing back and forth between them. I adjusted the paddle to return the serve.

"But, as you can see," I continued. "The way it's been programmed, it's literally impossible to win. The AI uses a formula to move its paddle, and the formula ensures that the paddle will always be in the perfect position."

"So don't bet any money is what you're saying." Kai sat in the chair beside me, a cold soda in his hands. He ran his fingers through his hair, staring intently at the game. "And you think we can do this in two hours?"

"Definitely. Pong isn't that complicated. Plus, we already have all the assets in the zip file." I slid over so Kai could take his position in front of the laptop.

It was strange to see Kai Taylor in my bedroom; like spotting a giraffe strolling down Main Street. Privately, I was worried about what he thought of my bedroom. Too small? Too geeky? Too *me*? Whatever his thoughts were, he kept them to himself.

I pointed to a prompt on the screen. "You'll want to follow these instructions. I'm here to give you tips if—"

"Mackayla?" Shaun's soft, sweet voice carried from the crack in my bedroom door. He pushed the door open and stepped inside, clutching an encyclopedia against his chest. His eyes were wet with tears.

"You okay?" I asked.

He sniffled. "The dinosaurs went extinct because of an asteroid. In Mexico. They all died. Mexico is close to here."

Close was a relative term, but I wasn't about to correct him. Shaun had a tendency to fall down rabbit holes. Recently, all of those rabbit holes ended at the same place: death. It was a morbid fascination for a boy of his age. Or any boy, really. It looked like dinosaurs were today's concern. I held my arms out to give him a hug. "That happened a long, long time ago. Millions of years ago. It's not going to happen again."

"That's not what Stephen Hawking said," Shaun mumbled. "He said that an asteroid was the biggest threat and that it might kill us all. And he was super duper smart. Super duper smarter than you."

Kai barked a laugh and tried to turn it into a cough.

I froze.

Right.

Kai.

I hadn't introduced Kai to Shaun, or prepped him in any way.

Shaun looked at Kai, noticing him for the first time. "Who are you?"

Anxiety pricked my skin. I wasn't sure I was ready for Kai to meet my brother. Shaun was the most important person in the world, and if anyone hurt him, I would come after them. Including Kai. That was the job of a big sister. If Kai made fun of him... I was already balling my fists at the thought.

"My name's Kai. I'm your neighbor." Kai smiled and turned to face Shaun. "You've been reading about asteroids?"

Shaun nodded hesitantly.

"At school, I learned that there's a whole group of scientists that look for large asteroids. They watch them for years to make sure they don't get close to earth. And right now, the next asteroid won't come anywhere near earth until 2095." Kai shrugged. "So you don't have anything to worry about."

Shaun looked puzzled. "Why wouldn't I have anything to worry about?"

"Because... umm..." Kai looked to me for help.

"Because the scientists will use their science to make sure the asteroid doesn't come close," I said. I had no idea if that was true or not. The only things I knew about asteroids came from cheesy old movies, and I highly doubted that NASA had plans to send a team of oil workers into space.

Shaun stopped sniffling. Wiped his eyes. And smiled.

Meltdown averted. It was a miracle.

"Okay," Shaun said. He stared at Kai, waiting for him to say something.

Kai scrambled, his gaze settling on Shaun's sneakers. "Steph Curry shoes?"

Shaun looked down at his sneakers, unfazed by the sudden conversation change. "Under Armor Curry 3 Mid Gs in Island Blue."

"Is he your favorite player?"

"He's the best player," Shaun said, his face lighting up. "He's the best shooter ever."

"No argument here," Kai said. He grinned. A real, genuine grin. "Did you know that, because he's so good at draining three-point shots, he changed the way people play basketball?"

Shaun pushed past me and sat in the chair next to Kai. He crossed his arms, a serious expression on his face. "How?"

Still holding my breath, I watched in amazement as the pair had a conversation about basketball that, admittedly, flew well over my head. Shaun was a shy kid, and that meant he never talked to strangers. Sometimes, he wouldn't even greet his grandparents. And yet, here he was, having a full conversation about basketball.

With Kai Taylor, of all people.

And Kai wasn't just indulging him – he seemed to actually enjoy the conversation. He was laughing, telling jokes, and treating Shaun as his equal. He didn't talk to him too slowly or too loudly, or just pretend he wasn't there. He engaged with him on his level. By the time their conversation was finished – twenty minutes later – Kai was Shaun's new hero.

Shaun skipped out of the room, leaving the door wide open.

I took a deep breath. "How did you—"

"He's a cool kid," Kai said. He said it a bit louder than he needed to – just loud enough so that his voice would carry to a certain someone who was probably stealthily standing outside my door, eavesdropping. Kai patted the chair beside him. "Come on. Let's play some pong."

12

KAI

*O*ne thing I learned from being grounded?

Saturdays without basketball, my friends, or even my cellphone sucked.

Big time.

I lay on my bed, tossing a mini basketball up in the air and catching it. Over and over.

For a week now, I'd been under total house arrest — save for school and my prison break to Mac's house the other night. Who knew that being tutored by the stubborn, sassy, and wonderfully strange girl-next-door would end up being the highlight of my week?

We'd had tons of fun making a game. Not only was Mac super smart, her sarcastic, snarky humor was hilarious. Plus, I'd loved meeting her family. Though our homes were practically identical from the outside, inside, Mac's house was everything mine wasn't — warm, messy, slightly chaotic, and homey. The walls were painted bright, sunny shades, there were report cards and finger paintings taped to the fridge, and the sink was full of dirty dishes.

In contrast, my house was all sharp, modern lines and

neutral color palettes. Neat as a pin. My dad barely left his office, and my mom was always out at parties and events.

I knew which I preferred.

I rolled off my bed with a sigh, and headed downstairs in search of something to eat.

In the kitchen, there was a note on the island, written in Mom's neat cursive lettering:

Gone to a dinner party at the Garretts' house. Back late.
Leftovers in the fridge if you're hungry.
BEHAVE!!!
Mom & Dad

Rude? Yes. But those were my parents. And their glittering social life had, for once, dealt me a lucky hand. I knew exactly how I wanted to play — I was going all in.

I ran back upstairs, showered, put on clean clothes, and snuck out the back door. Just in case.

In the backyard, I neatly scaled the dividing fence, landing heavily in a huge snow pile on the other side. I brushed myself off, walked to Mackayla's house, and casually knocked on her back door as if this was a totally normal, socially acceptable thing to do.

Footsteps came pattering towards me, and the door flew open.

"Hello, Kai Taylor!" Shaun's eyes lit up when he saw me. He didn't even look remotely surprised to see me, shivering and slightly breathless in his backyard.

"Hey, Shaun. Cool jersey." Today, Shaun was wearing an old Michael Jordan Bulls jersey that practically reached his ankles. His red hair was sticking up in all directions, and he was clutching a book entitled *The Last Great Viking Leader.*

"Who's better? Michael Jordan or Lebron James?"

I smiled. "Jordan."

Shaun closed the door.

I laughed and peered through the window, and there he

was on the other side, grinning. Apparently, the kid liked jokes.

"I take it back," I shouted. "Lebron's better."

Shaun opened the door. "You can come in, now."

"Thanks. Is your sister home?"

As if I had summoned her by magic, Mac rounded the corner. "Shaun, it's freezing, close the — Oh. What are *you* doing here?"

Mac stood by the back door dressed in Pacman pajama pants and an old t-shirt. Her hair was in a messy ponytail and she wore thick, black-rimmed glasses. For once, she wasn't wearing eyeliner. Her hands flew to her face, which exploded in a firetruck-red blush. Clearly, she wasn't expecting company.

I flashed her what I hoped was a winning smile. "Nice to see you too, Macgyver. And to answer your question, I'm here to take you to a party."

MAC

*K*ai Taylor was in my bedroom again.

He was sitting on my beanbag chair, watching me flip through my closet.

"I have nothing to wear to a stupid party," I grumbled. For once, I wasn't just saying something to get the banter flowing with Kai. I literally had no idea what to wear to a party at Hailey Danielson's mansion. I'd only been there once before – for a Halloween bash, when I'd had the luxury of hiding behind a costume.

Plus, nobody paid any attention to me back then.

Kai gracefully got to his feet. Why did he have to look so effortlessly cool? He was dressed in dark jeans, a tight, white t-shirt, and a faded, unbuttoned denim shirt, sleeves perfectly rolled up to show off his muscular forearms.

He came to stand beside me and peered into my closet. From this close proximity, I could feel the warmth of his skin, smell that intoxicating scent of his cologne.

Focus, Mackayla. This is Kai Taylor. You do not like him, no matter how much your body might be trying to tell you otherwise.

I grabbed a long-sleeved red skater dress — a gift from my girly-girl aunt that I'd never worn.

"This?" I asked skeptically. If there's one thing that pale, freckled redheads don't look great in, it's the color red.

Kai shook his head. "It's nice, it just… doesn't look like you. I told you before, you have awesome style. So, own who you are tonight instead of dressing like everyone else."

Turning away so he couldn't see my blush, I selected a top covered in neon graffiti print, and a black denim skirt with silver buttons on the front. "How about this?"

Kai sat down on the edge of my bed. Smiled. "Better. Especially if you wear those murder boots of yours."

"MURDER BOOTS?" I spluttered.

"Yeah, you know," Kai said. "Those purple ones you always wear."

I was incredulous. "You mean my Doc Martens?"

"Sure. Murder boots."

"Doc Martens have been around for over a century. They are beloved globally by millions of people."

Kai smirked. "I don't care what they're called. I just know that they look like they could do some serious damage if I say the wrong thing."

I couldn't help it. I laughed out loud.

"Murder boots," I mused. "I like it."

"You're gonna knock 'em dead." Kai raised his eyebrows. "Huh? See what I did there?"

"You and your stupid puns." I rolled my eyes, and headed to the bathroom to get changed.

Then, once I was safely out of his sight, I smiled.

AN HOUR LATER, we were standing on Hailey Danielson's front doorstep. If you could call it a doorstep — the place looked more like a palace than a family home.

I tugged at the hem of my skirt, anxious. Should I really have taken fashion advice from a boy? A boy that, until recently, had been my personal enemy number one?

Kai reached for the doorknob, but I held a hand up. "Wait, I need a minute."

"You look great," Kai told me, smiling that signature smile of his. He squeezed my hand. "You got this."

"Are you sure?"

"Positive."

We arrived inside a fancy lobby. Kai said that the party was in the basement, but there were still students milling around the main floor.

My heart dropped when I saw Madison, Lauren and Becca standing by the coat closet, hanging their jackets.

Lauren saw us first. She fluttered her eyelashes and tossed her blond ponytail. "Hello, Kai."

"Hi." Kai barely glanced at her. He turned to me. "Want me to take your coat?"

My coat currently felt like the only protective layer between me and my surroundings — a buffer. Maybe I could just wear it all night, be the Coat Girl. Perhaps I'd start a new trend.

Kai was doing that thing where he was looking at me like he could see inside my mind. He hung his coat up, then held out his hand in a "gimme" gesture.

"Hand it over, Macarena."

"Fine." I shook off my protective layer and passed it to him.

Madison watched our exchange, her green eyes gleaming. "That's an adorable choice of outfit, Mackayla. Very cute."

I looked up at Madison — literally, in her heels she towered over me. Her perfectly made-up face was smiling kindly. She wore tight leather pants, gold stilettos, and a busty top. Her dark hair was pulled up in an intricate braid crown. She looked like a freaking supermodel.

"Uh… thank you?" It was the first time Madison Albright had ever spoken to me. And I wasn't sure I liked it.

She nodded, graciously accepting my thanks.

"Oh, no problem. I think I used to own a skirt like that back in fifth grade. Absolutely precious that you've brought that back." She took a step towards me. Instinctively, I wanted to cower, but I held my ground. Then, she neatly sidestepped me. She came to a stop in front of Kai, and possessively ran a manicured fingertip down his chest. "And you?"

Kai raised his eyebrows. "What about me, Madi?"

"You look extra hot tonight, handsome. Find me later?"

Ah. This was her game. Use her charms to remove Kai from my side so that I ended up alone at this party. A fish out of water. Feeling ridiculous in my outfit she condescended, and wishing I had more friends.

Behind Madi, Becca and Lauren snickered.

Touché, Albright.

I took a deep breath and held it, fully expecting Madison's plan to play out as she wanted it to. Why would Kai slum it with me for the evening when Madison Albright had practically promised him a hook-up?

What I was *not* expecting was for Kai to step backwards, fix Madison with a dark-eyed glare and put his arm around me.

"Nah, Madi, I'm good." Kai's voice was ice cold. "I already have a date for this evening. And Mac looks absolutely gorgeous in what she's chosen to wear."

I could have pointed out that, technically, *he* had chosen my outfit. But my heart was beating too fast and my mouth was too dry to say anything. Kai Taylor had his arm around me, and I was loath to admit it, but I did not hate it one bit.

He felt strong, comforting, warm.

A protective barrier from all that could happen tonight.

14

MAC

By all counts, the party wasn't as bad as I'd anticipated.

Hailey Danielson's basement featured a huge games room, a mini movie theater, and a wet bar. The living area had been converted into a makeshift dance floor, and bass-thumping rap played through the state-of-the-art speakers.

Throughout the evening, Kai had been a perfect "date." He'd introduced me to his friends on the basketball team, partnered with me for games, and absolutely charmed the pants off Sofia and Noah. So much so that Sofia kept shooting me pointed looks when she thought Kai's back was turned.

Her judgement was terrible, however, and Kai caught her wiggling her eyebrows at me like an idiot several times. To his credit, he didn't say anything.

The only low spot at the party was Madison, who was shooting daggers at me from across the basement. That is, when she wasn't flirting with the entire defensive line of the football team and whispering to Lauren and Becca.

My stomach rumbled loudly and I considered asking Kai

where to find food. Unfortunately, he'd just gotten stuck into a game of darts with Hailey's boyfriend – Trey. Sofia and Noah were also out of the question as they were making out on one of the plush sectional sofas.

Not wanting to deal with Madison glaring at me anymore, I took this as my cue to set off in search of food. I wandered upstairs to the ginormous chef's kitchen.

The kitchen was empty, save for Hailey, Abby and Jordyn. Jordyn was sitting cross-legged on the kitchen island, inhaling an entire basket of chicken wings. She was dressed down compared to most girls at the party – wearing ripped jeans and a faded Broncos sweatshirt. Her blond hair was gathered in a sloppy ponytail.

Next to her, Abby leaned against the island, picking pineapple off a pizza slice. She was entirely more presentable in a cute, floaty pink top and white jeans.

Hailey had her head in the fridge. "I can't see any blue cheese. Is ranch okay?"

Jordyn rolled her eyes. "These are buffalo wings, Hailey. *Buffalo!* What do you think I am, some kind of savage?"

"You'll live." Hailey tossed the bottle of ranch dressing over her shoulder. Jordyn caught it deftly, flipped open the cap and dumped it all over her wings.

Hailey was still rolling her eyes when she closed the fridge door and turned back to her friends. As she turned, she spotted me hovering at the edge of the room like some kind of socially awkward hummingbird.

"Hey, Mackayla." The smile Hailey gave me was genuinely kind. She was so beautiful, with her long caramel hair and million dollar smile. She wore a short, midnight blue shift dress paired with black ankle boots. Effortlessly elegant and stylish, she looked every inch the perfect prom queen. Except for the teeny, tiny little problem that I was the nominee, not her.

"I'm so sorry about what happened," I blurted in response to her greeting.

Hailey's gaze flickered to her friends, then back to me. She shook her head. "You have literally nothing to be sorry about."

Jordyn wiped her mouth with the back of her hand, then gestured to the food. "You hungry?"

I walked towards the center of the kitchen, and Hailey passed me a paper plate. "Help yourself to anything."

Not daring to delve into wing territory, which clearly belonged to Jordyn, I grabbed a couple of pizza slices. Then, I stood next to Abby. She was the only one of the three I had ever really spoken to before. Although I knew tons about Jordyn from Sofia by default.

"I like your outfit," Hailey said. Her tone couldn't have been more different than the way Madison said the same sentence to me earlier. She was so sincere, I was a little shocked.

"I don't understand why you weren't nominated, Hailey," I blurted. "I didn't rig the vote, I swear."

There, I said it.

"Meh." Hailey shrugged. "Honestly, it's a good thing. It was really nice to see someone unexpected be nominated. And of course you didn't rig the vote."

"Are you really taking on Click?" Jordyn leaned forward, a smile playing on her lips.

I nodded hesitantly. "I think so."

Jordyn beamed approvingly. "About time someone did!"

"So, what's your plan?" Abby asked. She unscrewed the top of a bottle of soda and took a long drink.

I blinked. "Well, I'm not sure I can actually beat Madison — or you, of course, Jordyn — but I want to do something to put Click in its place. I know I was nominated as a joke, and I just want to show Evermore High that being different doesn't mean you're a joke. I'm so sick of this school and of everyone listening to Click's insidious lies all the time."

I was babbling like an idiot, but the girls were all smiling.

"Amen, sister." Jordyn held up a slightly saucy hand for a high-five. "And you don't have to worry about me. I'm not competing. I have no interest in prom, or poofy dresses, or Madison freaking Albright. In fact, as of right now, I am putting all of my support behind the Anti Prom Queen candidate."

My grin was a mile wide. "Really?"

Hailey nodded. "You have my full support, too. When Adam broke up with me, Click set out to destroy me. That app does nothing but give people a platform to bring others down and shame them publicly."

"Or, make them feel like they're not good enough because of who they are." Abby nodded. She'd been through the wringer with Click herself when she and Chase started dating.

"It's the worst thing that's ever happened to Evermore High." Jordyn's eyes blazed. "And I would like nothing better than to destroy it."

"So, what can we do to help?" Hailey leaned back against the countertop and crossed her legs at the ankle.

"So far, Kai Taylor — he's my neighbor — has been helping me."

Hailey smiled. "I like Kai. He's the nicest person on the basketball team, in my opinion."

Yet another unexpected revelation about Kai Taylor.

"Really?" I asked.

Hailey laughed at my skeptical expression. She cocked her head. "He's pretty hot too, don't you think?"

I blushed furiously.

"I mean… he's okay, I guess."

"OKAY?" Jordyn yelled, waving a half-eaten wing at me. A

mist of hot sauce sprayed the air around her. "That boy is like, smoking hot. And don't tell Dylan I said that."

We all burst out laughing.

"What's going on with you and Kai, anyway?" Abby asked.

"Nothing at all. I'm tutoring him in VGP, and he's helping me with this in return. Nothing more."

"Why?" Jordyn demanded.

I drummed my fingers against the kitchen counter, keeping time with my thrumming heartbeat. Why, indeed?

I thought Kai was hot, but so did every other girl in school.

I rolled my eyes. "Because he's Kai Taylor and I'm Mackayla Lafelle."

Jordyn tilted her head, confused. "What do you mean?"

"The biggest basketball star in the school, and the weirdo that got nominated for prom queen as a joke? It would be ridiculous."

Abby's face stretched into a slow, deliberate smirk. "More ridiculous than the nerdy school reporter dating the all-star quarterback?"

She had a point.

15

KAI

*S*omething insane had happened. Something absolutely and utterly and completely crazy.

I was actually looking *forward* to VGP class on Monday afternoon. Maybe it was because my skills were slowly improving, which meant I could potentially get the okay to play ball again soon.

Or, maybe, it was because of a certain feisty redhead.

The most interesting thing about Mac was that she had no idea how pretty she was, how good she'd looked in her skirt and top clothes. She had no idea how attractive her quirky personality was.

Not that I noticed those things. But I saw other people noticing them. Like any good friend would.

And, weren't we friends now? Kind of?

I wasn't sure what Mac thought of me these days. She seemed to hate me less than she used to. Plus, she sometimes even laughed at my jokes. Even my puns.

I walked into Mr. Vargas's classroom and my eyes were immediately drawn to Mac, sitting in the corner. Today, her red hair was pulled into a messy bun on top of her head, showing off her dangly, star-shaped earrings. She was wearing an oversized black and white plaid flannel shirt, baggy, ripped jeans, and, of course, her murder boots.

Mac looked up from her notebook and raised her eyebrows.

"Cool earrings."

"Thanks." She put a hand to one ear and looked at me expectantly, waiting for a punchline. But, I slid into my seat silently. Her glitter-lined eyes narrowed. "No ridiculous nickname?"

I flashed her a big smile. "Thought I'd give you the day off."

"What's the catch?" Mac knocked a boot against my sneaker under the desk.

"No catch, I'm just feeling generous."

Mac shook her head in disbelief, but I caught the twinkle in her eye as she turned away from me. The arrival of Mr. Vargas put an end to our conversation, and I sat up straight in my seat.

The basketball team had a big rivalry game coming up in a few days, and I needed to get back on that team. And that meant paying attention in class.

Today, we were supposed to make a simple platformer — like Mario. Basically, we had to create a series of pits and platforms for a cube to jump over. The key concept we were supposed to learn was incremental difficulty — which flew right over my head.

Fortunately, it did not fly over Mac's.

She leaned over and watched as I created another platform, then shook her head. "Your jumps are in the wrong order."

"How can they be in the wrong order?"

"Incremental difficulty," Mac said. "You always go from easy to hard. Think of each jump as a test that the player has to master. In the first jump, they have to make it over a pit. In the second jump, they have to make it over a longer pit. Then in the third jump, they have to jump over a longer pit and land between two saws."

She pointed to her game. "See?"

"Okay." I nodded. "I think I can do that."

At the end of the period, Mr. Vargas made his way to my desk.

"Okay, Mr. Taylor, let's have a look…"

16

MAC

*T*he classroom was so quiet you could've heard a pin drop. I held my breath, crossing my fingers behind my back. Mr. Vargas was bent over Kai's desk, playing the game. Kai was standing next to him, cracking his knuckles nervously.

After what felt like an eternity, Mr. Vargas stood up from playing Kai's game. "A-."

"What?" Kai stared down at Mr. Vargas, who was at least six inches shorter than he was. "Are you kidding?"

Mr. Vargas chuckled. "Mr. Taylor, I do not *kid* with my students."

"And I don't get A's." Kai shook his head, looking slightly dazed. His dark eyes glowed with hope. "Does this mean..."

Mr. Vargas nodded, smiling. "It does. The A- brings your average high enough that you can play on Friday."

Kai's face lit up in wonder, like a child on Christmas morning.

"Congratulations, Mr. Taylor. You've earned it."

"THANK YOU!" Kai pumped his fist in the air. He

grinned at Vargas, before spinning around to face me. "And Mac, thank YOU!"

Before I knew what was happening, I was in Kai Taylor's arms. He hugged me to his chest, lifted me off the ground, and spun me in circles. My arms instinctively tightened around his neck as he twirled me around. He was so tall, so solid, it was like I weighed nothing in his arms.

For just a moment, I let myself get swept away in the moment. I leaned into him, pressing my cheek to his warm chest. Breathed in his clean, woodsy scent. Focused on the feeling of his strong hands holding my body against him. My heart rate quickened, my breath became shallow. We were so close, close enough to...

And then, he set me down abruptly. So abruptly that I stumbled backwards.

Kai took a step backwards himself. Brushed off his t-shirt.

Our gazes connected.

"I, uh—" Kai said.

"Yeah, I, um..." I shook my head.

What was I trying to say? Hello, brain, anybody in there?

"Lunch," Kai stated, nodding vehemently. He reached for his laptop and backpack. "I need to meet Zane for lunch. Um... see you later?"

"Later," I mumbled.

Kai headed for the door and I watched his retreating figure, my head still foggy from his touch. My heart was thudding at a million miles per minute and I was sure I was the color of a nice, ripe tomato.

It took me a moment to realize Mr. Vargas had reap-peared next to me. Took me another to see that he looked way too amused by what had just played out.

He held out two tickets. "As promised, Mac. You did good."

I stared at him blankly for a beat, before realizing that I had to react. Be somewhat normal.

"Th– thanks." I reached for the tickets, my hands on autopilot. I opened my mouth to say something else, but nothing came out.

Apparently, my brain had left the building.

17

KAI

*P*laying in a rivalry game after two weeks of basketball exile was like finding an oasis in the Sahara desert. I ran out onto the court, proudly sporting my Panthers uniform, and took a moment to soak in the cheering crowd, the swell of the marching band music, and the heady smell of the freshly waxed floor.

I was officially ungrounded. My dad had released my phone from his custody, and I was here to win.

As I shot a few practice baskets before the game, I was pleased to see that my dry spell hadn't messed with my arm.

I was on top of the world.

Across the court, the Coaldale Cougars were doing their own warmup exercises while their coach bellowed at them, shooting spittle as he screamed. The Cougars were Evermore High's biggest rivals, making tonight's game nothing short of a grudge match. I wasn't worried, though. They had both a height and weight advantage, as a team, but I was sure we had better ball skills.

Next to me, Zane tossed a layup in the basket.

"Glad you're back, man." He jerked his head in the direction of the Cougars. "They look like they're out for blood."

As if on cue, the Cougars' center – who must've been 7-feet tall – glared at us and cracked his knuckles menacingly.

I was unimpressed. "We're gonna dance circles around those fools. And we have Mac to thank for that."

Zane cocked an eyebrow.

"The only reason I'm able to play tonight is because Mac helped me get my grades up," I clarified.

Zane dribbled the ball between his legs. "Well, tell her that me and the team are thankful. Is she here?"

He craned his neck, searching the bleachers.

"No, she doesn't do spor—" I cut myself off midsentence. Because Zane was pointing at the back row of the bleachers.

And there she was. Mac was sitting on the bleachers, looking around uncomfortably, her shoulders tense. Shaun was at her side, decked out in a Denver Nuggets jersey and eating a bucket of popcorn that was half the size he was. When he saw me looking, he stood up and waved.

I grinned and waved back like a maniac.

A smile passed over Mac's face as she watched my exchange with her little brother. When my eyes met hers, she shot me a thumbs up.

My heart tap danced against my will. Mackayla Lafelle — self-confessed organized-sports-hater and all around school-spirit killjoy — had come to watch me play.

I turned away slowly, a stupid grin still on my face. She probably wasn't here for me. Shaun just wanted to come. That was it.

Zane was watching me with amusement. "Dude, what's going on with you and the Anti Prom Queen girl?"

"Nothing." I took another shot. Missed.

Zane smirked. "Is she why you turned down Madison the other night?"

"Heard about that?"

"News travels fast."

"Apparently." I dropped a three. "There's nothing going on with me and Mac."

"Sure," Zane said. "Whatever you say."

I checked to see if any of the cheerleaders were in earshot. They were busy forming a pyramid at the end of the court, but I lowered my voice anyway. "There's nothing going on between me and Mac. I shot down Madison because she's trying to psych out Mac. She's mad people are taking Mac seriously."

"Isn't that what you wanted?"

I frowned — that was a weird question. Of course I wanted people to take Mac seriously. I shook my head. "I think she's got a shot."

Zane seemed confused for a beat. And then, he snorted. "Madi is a hot, popular senior. Going against her like that is stupid."

"Or brave," I snapped. "Look, this is a really good thing Mac is doing. She's taking a stand against bullying. Sending people the message that it's okay to be yourself. Jordyn Jones even said she wasn't going to campaign for queen, but give her full support to Mac."

"She did?"

"Didn't hear about that, huh?"

Zane, shocked into a rare silence, looked impressed. Pride bloomed in my chest for Mac, and I snuck a look at the bleachers to see if she was still watching me.

She was.

MAC

$\mathcal{I}$n early February, arctic temperatures and nasty blizzards gave way to a spell of perfect winter weather. Cool, crisp days filled with blue skies and sunshine sent hordes of people rushing to the nearby ski hills every weekend.

Compared to January, the warmer temperatures made for ideal after-school walking conditions. But, for some strange reason, Kai Taylor was still offering me rides home after school.

And, even stranger, I kept accepting these offers.

And I maybe even looked forward to our new after-school routine.

"Ready to go, Mac Miller?" Kai smiled from the driver's seat as I jumped in his car on a Thursday afternoon.

"Who?" I asked as I buckled my seatbelt.

"Who?!" Kai put a hand on his heart, shocked. "Only one of the greatest rappers of a generation. Gone far too soon."

"I've never heard of him," I said carefully. Kai's face was uncharacteristically solemn. "I don't listen to rap music."

"Well that's just plain wrong of you," Kai said. He reached

for his phone, scrolled through Spotify. "Let me give you an education."

A moment later, blaring rap filled the car. He shifted the car into gear and backed out of his parking space. After a few breaths, he looked over, raised an eyebrow.

"Okay, okay," I said. "It's not bad."

"Not bad?"

"It's... good," I grudginging conceded.

Kai flashed me a winning smile. "So, who was right?"

"Not answering that." I laughed. "And how many hours a day do you spend thinking up those nicknames for me, anyway?"

Kai turned down the volume a touch and side-glanced at me. "Let's just say Google is my best friend."

As I laughed, a weird, warm feeling creeped across my skin. It was a feeling I'd been getting often when I was around Kai these days.

As much as I complained about the nicknames, my stomach filled with butterflies at the thought that Kai spent his spare time thinking them up for me. That he thought of me when he listened to his favorite rapper.

That he thought about me at all.

Back when I'd hated Kai from a distance, I'd seen him as two-dimensional — a stereotypical, jerky jock. But, as I got to know him, it seemed that there was another pleasant surprise at every turn. Surprises that tilted my view of him, helped me see my neighbor through a new lens. As a... friend?

Or maybe more.

I shook my head, trying to get that particular dumb thought out of my head. Kai would never be interested in me.

"What are you thinking about?" Kai asked, looking amused.

Time for a serious subject change.

"I've been thinking about Valentine's Day," I said as Kai pulled out of the parking lot.

"Got a hot date?" Kai quirked an eyebrow.

"Hardly." I flushed. I looked down at my hands and picked at my chipped nail polish. "No, I was thinking about those stupid Candygrams they do at school."

The annual day of public love and affection was less than a week away, which meant that Evermore High's signature Candygrams booth would return for another year. The booth allowed students to send heart-shaped lollipops to one another — all to raise funds for prom, of course. But to me? The Candygrams booth was just another way for Evermore High students to wedge a further gap between who was popular and who was not.

"What about them?" Kai asked as he braked at a red light. He was the kind of person who received multiple lollipops every year, despite probably sending none at all.

"I hate the way Click uses the booth as an opportunity to prey on people who don't get Candygrams."

Kai nodded slowly. "That's true… I guess it does allow Click to be a bully and make people feel bad about themselves."

"Exactly." I picked at my thumbnail, scraping off a piece of glittery polish. "It's like ranking people's worth based on who gets a Candygram and who doesn't. In reality though, it's just a piece of pink candy that means nothing. I wish everyone could get one so the entire student body would feel loved on a day that makes so many people feel terrible about themselves."

Kai suddenly smacked the steering wheel, making me jump.

"You know what, Bernie Mac?" He turned to me, a grin slowly spreading across his face. A white-toothed, confident, sexy grin that made my insides flip over.

"What?"

"I think I have an idea…"

STRINGS OF PAPER hearts decorated the corridors. Pink and red cards were taped on locker doors. All around the school, girls carried teddy bears and balloons and flowers, glowing with pride.

Like the Black Plague, Valentine's Day was well and truly inescapable in the confined space that was Evermore High.

Only this year, I was actually excited for what was going to play out.

By the time lunch came around, I was a bundle of anticipation. I hopped from foot to foot as I stood in line for food, then grabbed the first things I saw — a pita wrap and an apple. I made a beeline for Sofia and Noah, who were sitting at a table in the center of the cafeteria.

I slid onto the bench seat across from the happy couple. "What's up, lovebirds?"

Sofia beamed and held out her hand. A delicate, silver bracelet dangled from her wrist. "Did you see what Noah got me?"

"It's beautiful," I told her, then turned to Noah. "Well done."

Noah laughed. "Thank you, Mac. It only took me, like, five trips to the mall to find the right one."

Of course. Noah loved Sofia so much he'd probably go to Mars if she asked.

Over the tannoy, the tinny voice of Principal Potter filled the room. "Happy Valentine's Day, Evermore High! Who's ready for a visit from this year's cupids?"

Cheers erupted around the cafeteria.

"Are you ready?" Sofia squeezed my hand.

I nodded. Excitement squirmed in the pit of my stomach. "I think so."

I took a quick glance around and located Kai. He was sitting a few tables away with a bunch of his teammates and cheerleaders. He caught my eye, and gave me a thumbs up.

I bit my lip.

Music played through the speakers, and the entire school population began screaming and cheering as Coach Clarence, the football coach, and Mr. Adebayo, the English teacher, strutted into the cafeteria. They wore bedsheets fashioned into togas, and costume fairy wings over their clothes. In their arms were huge tubs of Candygrams.

The football players leaped to their feet, hooting and hollering. Boys whistled and catcalled, while girls screamed and squealed. It was insanity.

Mr. Adebayo did a twirl.

Once the cheering finally calmed down, names were announced.

The usual suspects were announced first. Madison Albright received a whole armful of lollipops. As did Chase, Hailey and Dylan. Trey Carter scowled all the way to the front to collect his numerous Candygrams from his fans, while Hailey snapped photos, laughing. Noah was called to the front to receive his own stack of lollipops, ducking his head as he went. Kai was next. On his way back to his table, arms overflowing, he caught my eye again and winked.

Soon, all of the athletes, student council and popular crowd had been called up. But, the buckets of Candygrams remained plentiful.

Without hesitation, Mr. Adebayo continued down his list. And, name by name, people stood to collect their lollipops.

My heart warmed to see the shock and subsequent smiles on the faces of the students who had never previously received a Candygram. They made their way to the front, blushing and shaking their heads in confusion.

Whispers began to whirl around the cafeteria as more names were called.

And more names.

And it continued on like this until every single student in the cafeteria had a Candygram. Until every last student had a smile on their face.

Click remained conspicuously silent throughout the entire thing. It was beautiful.

I was so caught up in the moment, I barely noticed Kai appear beside me.

"High-five, partner!" He held up a hand as he flopped into the seat next to mine. I smacked it as hard as I could. We'd actually pulled it off. Around the cafeteria, people were whispering excitedly, snapping selfies and tearing into their lollipops.

Kai gave Noah a fistbump. "Thanks for your help, dude. This is amazing."

Noah shook his head. "I did nothing. It was a great idea."

"Kai's pretty smart." I lightly elbowed him in the ribs, enjoying watching his cheeks turn pink. He deserved all the credit for this idea — sending a Candygram to everyone in school with a note inside that read: *With love from the Anti Prom Queen.*

Step two of his plan for my prom queen campaign was to get involved in a school event and show some school spirit. And what better way to deliver that than with Valentine's candy? Plus, we'd kept everyone safe from Click's tormenting for the time being. Noah, whose Dad was a famous Hollywood director, had generously funded "Operation Feel the Love" – as we'd nicknamed it.

After the Candygram event ended, Mr. Adebayo and Coach Clarence left the cafeteria to a standing ovation. Electricity and positive energy buzzed through the room. Love was well and truly in the air.

I was still beaming when Sofia looked at me quizzically. "Where's yours?"

"Where's my what?"

"Your Candygram, silly."

"Oh!" I laughed, realization dawning on me. "I was so busy setting this up, I guess I forgot about myself."

"I didn't," a warm voice said behind me.

I spun around to the sight of Kai holding out a pink lollipop, smiling slightly bashfully.

"You got me one?" My voice came out embarrassingly croaky.

He nodded silently. Across from him, Sofia clapped her hands together.

"Open the note, Mac."

I unrolled the little piece of paper attached to my Candygram.

Macaroni,

Will you be my date to the Valentine's dance?

From your not-so-secret admirer.

When I looked up, Kai was looking right at me. His dark eyes burned into mine so intensely that I forgot to breathe.

Or speak.

"Well?" Kai finally asked.

There was a lump in my throat.

"It's part of your Anti Prom Queen duties to turn up at those things, remember?" he added.

Right. My Anti Prom Queen campaign.

I swallowed hard. Nodded. Of course, this was all part of his strategy to help me with my campaign. That was all.

"Yes, I'd love to." The tension in the air was heavy like a wool blanket.

"Cool, well, uh… good. Yup. Guess I'd better get to class." Kai got to his feet and grabbed his backpack.

"You made everyone really happy today, Kai."

He shot me a humble half-smile. "You gave me the idea. Need a ride home after school?"

I nodded.

"See you then," he said softly.

"See you then."

As Kai walked away, Sofia shook her head slowly. "Oh girl, you got it baddddddd," she sang.

For once, I didn't try to argue. Or throw food at her.

Instead, I watched him go. My hand was still warm from his touch.

KAI

"*D*id you know that St. Valentine was a Catholic saint who was executed by Emperor Claudius II in the third century A.D.?" Shaun beamed.

"I didn't, buddy." It was Friday night, and I was in Mackayla's living room, picking her up for the Valentine's Dance at school. I'd never been nervous picking up a date for a school dance before. But tonight, my heart was banging like a drum in anticipation.

Shaun nodded, his face darkening. "And did you also know that, before it was St. Valentine's Day, February 14th was a Roman pagan festival where they would sacrifice goats?"

"Oh, I didn't know that either." I looked down at Shaun, whose lower lip was wobbling.

"Why would they do that, Kai Taylor? Goats are nice."

By now, I knew the drill: when in doubt, distract Shaun like crazy. "That was a very long time ago, buddy. Nobody sacrifices goats anymore. People love goats, and there are even Youtube videos of them making funny noises. Have you ever seen those?"

Shaun's eyes widened. "Show me."

I pulled my phone out of my suit pocket, and took a seat on the couch. Shaun climbed right into my lap, the threat of tears averted for now. I pressed play on the screaming goat video and Shaun watched, eyes wide.

Mac's mom came into the room and smiled at the sight of Shaun giggling at the video. "Thanks for keeping Shaun entertained, Kai. Mac's almost ready. Can I get you some water or anything while you wait?"

I shook my head. "I'm good thanks, Mrs. Lafelle."

Shaun looked up. "Are you sure you're not Mac's boyfriend?"

"Shh, leave him alone, Shaun."

My head jerked up at the sound of the familiar voice. And the sight in front of me almost left me speechless.

"Wow," I breathed, following Shaun in scrambling to my feet. Mackayla stood in front of me, dressed in a knee-length black velvet dress. Her hair was in a cascade of long red curls, pinned back on one side with a purple flower clip. Her hazel eyes were framed by smokey eye makeup, and she'd swapped out her murder boots for silver, strappy sandals. "You look incredible."

I extended a hand to her, and Mac's pale skin glowed pink as she slipped her hand into mine. "You don't look so bad, yourself."

I chuckled. She was the same Mac, just dressed fancier.

And I was here for it.

"You look like a princess, Mac," Shaun said reverently.

I didn't take my eyes off her for a second. "She really does."

♥

THE DANCE WAS in full swing by the time we arrived. The school gym had been transformed with the help of a thousand glimmering fairy lights and hundreds of heart-shaped helium balloons. A stage was set up in one corner, and Trey Carter's band — Stonewash Sunrise — were performing a series of love ballads. In another corner, tables were laden with cookies, chocolate treats and a big bowl of bright-red punch that the staff volunteers watched with hawk eyes.

The basketball court served as a dance floor, and beautifully-dressed couples swayed, bodies close together, to the sound of Trey's gravelly vocals. The guy was super talented, to say the least.

Mac and I hovered in the doorway for a moment.

"Want to dance?" I asked, my voice cracking slightly.

Since when had I been so nervous around my neighbor?

Thankfully, Mac nodded. "Okay, then."

I took her hand and led her to the middle of the dancefloor. Hesitated for a second before placing my hands on her waist. "This okay?"

She nodded again. Then, she put her hands stiffly on my shoulders.

I ran my tongue along my bottom lip. This was painfully awkward.

But then, I caught Mac's eye. I smiled. She smiled back.

A look of understanding passed between us, and we both began to laugh. My tension melted like snow in the sunshine. Everything was okay. Mac's arms circled my neck, and, filled with renewed confidence, I pulled her a little closer. We began to dance.

"Hi." She looked up at me, her hazel eyes searching mine. The scent of vanilla body lotion mingled with minty mouthwash, and my gaze came to rest on her lips. Pink, smiling lips. I suddenly had an urge to kiss those lips.

A clinically insane urge.

What was wrong with me tonight? This was Mac. She didn't want to kiss me.

"Hi," I whispered back, trying and failing to sound casual.

"Do you think we're going to be all over Click by the end of the night?"

Around the gym, people were stealing glances at us. Taking pictures. "I guess that was part of the plan? We're making sure people know you're present at school social events. Which means, inevitably, ending up on Click."

"I think I'm okay with that." Mackayla moved towards me a little more, her pretty eyes dancing.

Was she... *flirting* with me? My heart rate picked up.

"So very dedicated to the cause of taking down Click." I grinned.

Mac's playful expression hardened. What had I said wrong? I opened my mouth but, before I could say a word, Mac let out a huge sigh. "Can I tell you something, Kai?"

"Anything," I said. I meant it.

"This whole 'taking down Click' thing... I'm not just doing it for me. Frankly, I don't really care that some idiot nominated me as a joke prom queen, or that Click posted a gross photo of me."

"I know, Mac." I gently tilted her chin upwards, forcing her eyes to meet mine. "You're amazing. Look at the good you're doing — you want to help other students who feel victimized or bullied by Click."

Mac's lip trembled, and she shook her head slightly. "Not just other students."

Realization struck me like an arrow to the heart.

"Shaun?" I asked.

Mac nodded, casting her gaze to the ground one more. "He's so... good. So innocent. He sees the best in everyone. People aren't going to understand who he is, they're going to judge him and make fun of him for being different. And, if

Click is still running the show by the time he gets to Ever-more High, this place will eat him alive. Imagine what Click would do to him, Kai."

Mac hiccupped, and I tightened my arms around her. She rested her head against my chest.

"You are the best person I've ever met," I whispered into her hair. "The best big sister Shaun could have ever asked for. You always stand up for what's right, you defend the under-dog. I love that about you. We are going to take down Click once and for all. For Shaun."

Mac looked back up at me, her eyes teary. "For Shaun."

She glanced around, then swiped her eyes furiously. "And speaking of Click, literally everyone is staring."

I took a quick scan of the gym. She was right. People weren't just casually watching and taking pictures anymore — they were staring, openmouthed. We were under the microscope, our every move being examined.

I just wanted to be alone with her, away from all of this.

"I have an idea," I said. "Come with me…"

MAC

"*W*here are we going?"

"You'll see." Kai tugged my hand, leading me down the dimly-lit corridor towards the... Boys' locker room?!

I whacked Kai on the arm with my free hand. "Ew, Taylor. If you think I'm going to hide out in your locker room all night, you have another thing coming."

"Please, have some faith in me. I'm not taking you to the locker room." Kai stopped outside the locker room door, looked around to check that the coast was clear, then pulled me inside.

For a moment, we were in complete darkness. I was still clutching Kai's hand, painfully aware of his closeness, the tingle that shot down my spine when his sleeve brushed against my bare arm.

Then, he flipped on the lights, and the room was bathed in fluorescent light. I looked up at Kai and immediately stepped sideways, putting some space between us. Looking at him made me feel a little lightheaded. He looked so good

— too good — in that dark navy suit jacket and white shirt, unbuttoned at the collar.

I quickly looked away, flustered.

And then, I took in the Evermore High boys' locker room in all of its glory. The sight of this mythical place — the stuff of Evermore legends — was… well, disappointing.

It looked exactly how you'd imagine a boys' locker room would look — faded yellow paint on the walls, a damp, humid shower area, endless laundry bins, and black and silver team jerseys hanging in little cubbies. The humid air was tinged with the scent of stale sweat.

Gross.

"I don't know if I have any faith in you, Taylor." I shook my head. "This sure looks like you've taken me to the locker room."

Kai smiled mysteriously. "This isn't our final destination."

At the very back of the room, there was a window above a bench. Kai jumped up on the bench and pushed the window open. "Trust me?"

"Nope," I said. But I climbed onto the bench next to him.

"Good to hear." He grinned wickedly.

The window faced out onto a metal platform below. Kai launched himself through, landing with the grace of a gazelle on the platform outside. He beckoned to me to follow.

I hesitated. "I'm wearing a dress."

"I promise I won't look," Kai said.

I screwed up my face, assessing the situation.

"Turn around," I instructed. He did.

Then, I took a deep breath, hitched up my skirt, and began to climb out of the window. What was I doing, sneaking around the school with Kai Taylor late at night? And where, oh where, were we going?

I wanted to find out.

I pulled myself through the window and clumsily hopped down on the other side, landing awkwardly in my sandals.

"Can I look now?" Kai called.

"Yup." I brushed myself off, then wrapped my arms around myself. It was freezing out here, and my skin erupted in goosebumps.

Quick as a flash, Kai shrugged off his suit jacket and draped it around my shoulders. It was massive on me, but warm. It smelled like him.

"Come on then, Mackayla." He held out his hand.

I flushed as I took it. "Since when do you call me Mackayla?"

"Since no nickname could possibly live up to how you look tonight." Kai smiled.

My heart did a somersault, but I shook it off. He probably said stuff like that to all the girls.

"Come on," he said, leading me along the platform to what looked like a fire escape.

"Where are we going?" I whispered.

"Up."

We climbed four flights of stairs and then walked out onto the roof. My breath caught in my throat. The sky was a velvety blanket of stars, shining bright above the silhouette of the mountains in the distance. The lights of the town of Evermore twinkled in the valley below.

We must've been standing directly above the gym because the faint tones of a love song carried through the night air. It was... magical.

"Whoa," I breathed.

"I come up here sometimes to think." He smiled, pleased with my reaction. "It's kind of my secret spot."

"It's incredible." I looked up to see him watching me intently. His dark eyes glimmered in the starlight as his gaze moved over me. Heat rose in my cheeks.

"Do you want to dance, Mackayla?" He moved a little closer to me.

My head swam and I felt weightless. "You want to dance with me? Up here?"

He stepped closer still. "I thought it might be nicer without everyone watching."

I nodded, and Kai pulled me towards him. Wrapped his arms around me. Even in just his thin shirt, his body was warm against mine. We began to sway together.

"What do you think about when you come up here?" I asked.

Kai didn't respond for a moment, his face clouding over in thought. When he did finally talk, his voice was carefully playful. "You know… girls, basketball, how to take over the world."

I raised my eyebrows at him.

"And girls," he added.

"You already said girls."

"I guess I think about girls the most." Kai flashed me that confident, flirty smile he always wore around school. The one that made all the girls go weak in the knees, the one that used to drive me crazy with annoyance.

But I was beginning to think that smile was a facade. Armor.

I didn't return Kai's signature smile. Instead, I held his gaze solemnly.

"Are you going to tell me what you *really* think about when you come up here?" I asked softly.

Something in his dark eyes shifted. He gathered me closer to his chest, breaking our eye contact as he did so. It was a move, I realized. A way to avoid my question, dodge the bullet. He wasn't going to open up to me.

But then, he began to talk. "I think about all of my responsibilities. The pressure I'm under from my dad, from my coach, from the school, to excel. Basketball is the only thing I've ever been good at, and if I keep messing everything else up, I'll lose it. And then what?"

I shook my head against his chest. "You won't. You're so much smarter than anyone gives you credit for — including yourself."

"I dunno about that, Mac." His voice was sadder than I'd ever heard it. "I'm good for one thing and one thing only. And, for two weeks, when basketball was taken from me and I couldn't play, I'd never felt more useless in my life. I let my team down, let my dad down. Click berated me. Basketball is all anyone cares about when they see me, when they talk to me. My parents included. And it just makes me think... if I wasn't a good ball player, would anyone even like me? Would anybody want to be around me?"

I remembered the insults his father had hurled at him, how Click had called him stupid, and my heart cracked for Kai. To cope with the pressure of always having to perform, he had built sarcastic, cocky walls around himself that were a mile high. He kept everyone out. But, little by little, he was allowing me through those walls, showing me what was really inside.

And I liked everything I saw.

I tilted my chin upwards and met his eyes. "I would."

Kai's eyes glowed a little brighter.

"That means a lot," he said, his voice hoarse.

Our gazes locked together and he ran his index finger along the side of my face. The move made me shiver.

My breathing became shallow as he slowly leaned towards me.

I leaned in, too. Closer, closer...

Buzz!

Buzz!

The noises of our vibrating phones cut through the air

like a knife. We sprang apart like we'd been electrocuted. I stared at Kai, wide-eyed. Touched my fingertips to my lips.

Had that really almost happened?

Kai smiled, more shaky than usual. He exhaled loudly. "I'll give you one guess who that is."

My face darkened. Only one thing could possibly have the power to ruin our moment.

"What does Click have to say this time?" I snarled.

MAC

"*M*orning!" Shaun yelled, cannonballing onto my bed. He began jumping up and down. "Wake up, wake up, wake up!"

"Noooooo," I moaned, pulling my pillow over my head.

But, I was smiling.

Last night was amazing. Kai had been the perfect date. And every moment I spent with him, I found myself liking him just a little bit more. I'd initially thought that someone like Kai could never, ever like a girl like me, but he'd almost kissed me last night. I was sure of it.

After our phones went off, rudely interrupting our almost-kiss, we agreed not to check the Click blast. Whatever it said, it wasn't important.

Shaun ran out of my room, and I rolled over in bed and grabbed my phone. The lock screen showed three Click blasts — I ignored those, too — and what I'd hoped to see: a message from Kai.

Click's going crazy, he texted. *What do you say we ditch our phones for the day and escape somewhere?*

Anticipation zipped up my spine at the thought of a day

alone with Kai. I sat up straight in bed, threw my covers off and jumped to my feet before texting him back.

Two hours later, we climbed out of Kai's Audi at the Colorado Convention Center in downtown Denver. Outside the Convention Center, a behemoth banner read "GameON Video Game Expo" in neon, pixelated lettering.

My heart skipped a couple of beats. We were actually here!

Kai glanced up at the banner, then looked at me.

"Think we're in the right place?" he asked.

I shoved him.

He grinned.

My knees went weak.

In his black, fitted tee, backwards baseball cap and Ray-Bans, Kai looked like a superstar athlete keeping a low profile en route to the stadium. He did not look like a teenage boy about to attend a video game convention.

"Any words of wisdom before we go in?" he asked as we stepped into the line. Around us, other patrons were in full cosplay, representing their favorite video game characters. Kai didn't bat an eyelid, he took the whole thing in his stride. Like he had when he met Shaun.

"Maybe don't be yourself," I teased.

This time, he shoved me. But gently. And just as soon as he pushed on my shoulder, he put his hand on my back to steady me.

He gathered me into his arms. "I'm actually kind of excited, never been to one of these thingies before."

A couple in front of us dressed like Princess Zelda and Link turned and stared.

"You haven't?" Link asked. He was about 5'6" and skinny as a rail. His face was absolutely incredulous. "GameON is a mind-blowing place to start. We had to camp out overnight to get tickets."

"Really?" Kai leaned back against the guardrail and folded his arms.

Zelda nodded so vigorously her tiara almost fell off. "Tickets to GameON are like gold dust. How did you guys get yours?"

Kai looked sideways at me, his face twisting into an indecipherable expression.

"We won them," I said.

Link whistled through his teeth. He looked at Kai. "Dude, you have no idea how lucky you are."

The line began to move, and Link and Zelda waved their goodbyes as they were moved forward to the final queuing area. The second they were gone, Kai rounded on me. "Why didn't you tell me?"

I was taken aback by his angry tone. "Tell you what?"

"That this was such a big deal."

I shrugged. "It's not that big of a deal."

"Oh yeah?" Kai rubbed his forehead, looking unreasonably upset. "Then tell me you didn't try and get your own tickets before Mr. Vargas hooked you up."

"Of course I tried. They were impossible to get." I threw up my hands, exasperated. "What is going on with you right now?"

Kai looked at me for a moment, his lips pressed into a thin line. Then, his dark eyes softened.

"I'm sorry. I'm not mad or anything," he said. His voice was uncharacteristically small and quiet. "I just don't think I'm the right person to be here with you. Why are you wasting your spare ticket on me?"

Ah.

I looked up at Kai. His dark eyes were filled with conflict and confusion. I could see what he was feeling: he wanted to be here, but he didn't want me to waste something important on him.

Once again, my heart lurched painfully for Kai. He was caught between two worlds — on the one hand, he was the boy that every guy wanted to be. But, he also lived in a world where he truly believed nobody wanted to be around him or cared about him for the person he was.

"I didn't waste it." I shook my head vehemently. "I didn't even consider taking anyone else. I wanted to share this with you."

Kai looked skeptical. "Serious?"

"Cross my heart." I drew a little X over my chest.

Without a beat of hesitation, Kai bent down and pressed a kiss to my forehead. His warm lips met my cool skin for just a moment, but my entire body erupted in shivers.

"Thank you, Mackayla," he said softly.

The line began to move again. I took a deep breath, and shook myself out of my daze. "Are you ready?"

My favorite cocky grin was back. "I was born ready."

22

MAC

*W*e played demos of futuristic, interplanetary shooting games. We donned VR headsets and entered a virtual battle arena to duel with a giant troll. We ran around a massive Pac-man maze, and drove race cars around the Formula 1 track in Monaco. Kai tried on a pink bikini top and a mermaid tail in a simulation fashion show, and I didn't think I'd ever laughed so hard in my life.

GameON was better than I could've anticipated. The lights were brighter, the crowd was buzzier, and the games were beyond my wildest imagination. But it wasn't any of those things that made GameON so special. In fact, it wasn't a thing at all.

It was a person.

I was browsing one of the shopping stalls when I realized I'd lost Kai. As the teller rang up my new t-shirt — with the words "I Paused My Game to Be Here" — I craned my neck to look for him.

I spotted him about 30 feet away, standing at a silver and blue booth. He was locked in an intense conversation with a huge dude whose arms were tattooed in sleeves and a pierced lip. Kai's eyes were shining passionately.

Huh?

As I made my way over, Kai saw me and beckoned me forward. "Mac! Mac, come here!" He gestured at the man like they were lifelong besties. "I'd like you to meet Milton Hicks."

I stuck out my hand automatically, and Milton shook it. "Kai has been telling me a lot about you, Mac."

"He has?" I gaped.

"Says you're a talented coder."

I smiled shyly at Milton. "I don't know about that."

"Milton's company is having a video game design competition!" Kai practically shouted. He was hopping up and down excitedly, radiating enthusiastic energy. "You have to enter, Mac."

My eyes widened. "Really?"

For the first time, I noticed what was printed on Milton's t-shirt – a blue, shimmery, circular logo that read *Electric Slide Games.*

No FREAKING way.

"You work for ES Games?" I could barely contain my excitement. My eyes were probably literal cartoon-heart eyes, I was fangirling so hard.

"Sure do." Milton nodded. "I'm here at GameON to recruit people to sign up for our competition. It's open to all up-and-coming game designers. Participants are asked to make a prototype of an original game. Deadline is the end of May and the winner gets a summer internship at ES."

Could this day get *any* better?

"Where and when do I sign up?" I blurted.

Milton laughed. Passed me a tablet. "Right here, and right now."

A few minutes later, I walked away from the Electric Slide booth feeling like I was floating on air.

"Best. Day. Ever," I declared.

"You're totally going to win," Kai said.

I shook my head. "I don't know, I'm sure they get tons of talented people signing up."

Kai shrugged. "So? You're talented, too."

We meandered towards the edge of the expo, no real direction in mind. I was happy soaking everything in. It was a little quieter over here, away from the throb of the crowds clustered at the central exhibitions. We made our way past old arcade games, a cluster of kids' games, and a Dance Dance Revolution competition.

"Hey, what's this?" Kai pointed to a curtain-flanked, old-school booth in the corner. The exterior was covered in pictures of swirling train tracks.

The booth attendant smiled. "Want a go? You build your own rollercoaster, then try it out in a simulation."

"Uh, YES!" Kai shouted. He grabbed my hand. "Come on!"

I giggled as he tugged me along. "I'm guessing you like rollercoasters?"

He turned around and looked me right in the eye. "No better thrill."

At his words, my stomach dropped into freefall. I didn't need a rollercoaster simulation with Kai Taylor around — my insides produced the same sensation all on their very own.

We ducked into the booth, and the attendant closed the curtain behind us. "Have fun!"

Inside the booth, there were two side-by-side gaming seats, along with a tablet and a giant screen. On the tablet, you could swipe through rollercoaster parts and select them to build your own track. We started with the steepest hill we could find, then found a couple helixes, a loop, and another hill.

Finally, we were finished. Our very own rollercoaster: The Scream Queen.

We buckled into our seats.

"Are you ready?" Kai asked.

"I was born ready," I shot his line back at him.

"You can do the honors."

I pressed play on the tablet. The lights in the booth dimmed. On the giant screen in front of us, huge letters appeared telling us to "get ready for the ride of a lifetime."

Kai reached over and brushed his fingers against mine, sending an electric current through my skin. "Scared?"

Our seats jolted backwards. I squealed.

On the screen, we began to climb.

"Terrified," I admitted.

His fingers wove through mine. We climbed higher.

"Hold on tight!" We'd reached the apex, the ground a distant blur hundreds of feet below. On the screen, our cart went up and over the top of the coaster. We paused for a split second of delicious anticipation at the peak, hovering at the top of the world.

Then, we plunged into the abyss.

"AGGGGGGH!" I screamed, clutching Kai's hand as our seats tipped forward, air blowing in our faces as we came crashing downwards at what felt like real, breakneck speed.

On the screen, the world around the coaster was a blur as we took a sharp corner, almost sending me toppling on top of Kai. We took another, and another, dipped and spun and swirled and soared until I was dizzy with adrenaline and laughter.

By the time our cart pulled back into the station on the screen, my head was spinning, every sense tingling. Exhilaration rushed through my veins as I turned to Kai.

"Oh my gosh, that was—"

He silenced me with a kiss.

Just the softest graze of his lips against mine, but it was enough to send fire through my body. He retreated slightly, and our eyes locked for a long, long moment before he brought his mouth to mine again, plunging me into freefall once more. I circled my arms around his neck, pulling him closer to me. He tangled his hands in my hair in response, kissing me and kissing me until I was completely breathless.

When we finally broke apart, he smiled a smile so gorgeous, it hurt my stomach.

"I've wanted to do that for a while." He looked at me from under half-closed eyelids and bit his bottom lip.

"Me too," I stuttered, still seeing stars.

Kai cupped my face in his hands, touched his forehead to mine.

"Best. Day. Ever," he whispered softly, and his lips met mine again.

23

MAC

I usually hated Mondays. Mostly thanks to first period Gym class followed by a double period of Chem and AP Algebra.

Gross.

But, this was no regular Monday.

"Mackayla!" Kai's voice echoed through Evermore's hallways. I was standing at my locker, switching out textbooks.

He jogged right up to me, smiling big. He was dressed for basketball practice already. He wore a Panthers Basketball hoodie and gray sweatpants that somehow made him look even hotter than usual.

"Hi," I said, dropping my head. I felt almost shy. I hadn't seen Kai since he dropped me home on Saturday night with a lingering kiss. But, we'd spent the rest of the weekend texting.

"Missed you." Kai wrapped me in a hug and my heart sped up. A vicious little voice had been hissing doubts at me all day, telling me that, at school, things would be different. That Kai wouldn't want to be seen with me. Wouldn't want people to know we'd kissed.

But here he was, putting his arms around me in the hallway for all to see. Like it was the most normal, natural thing in the world.

"Hungry?" Kai smiled down at me.

I stepped out of his embrace and slammed my locker shut. "Starved."

"Come on, then." He held out his hand. I took it. And, together, we walked to the cafeteria.

Kai chattered away, oblivious to the hundreds of gawking stares around the cafeteria. Every pair of eyes in our immediate vicinity was locked on our intertwined hands.

When we sat down a few minutes later at an empty table, Kai looked at me quizzically. "You're unusually quiet today."

"Are you trying to say I'm usually loud?"

Kai took a big bite of pepperoni pizza. Chewed. Swallowed. "No?"

I swatted his arm. "I don't mean to be quiet, I'm just a bit freaked out. I don't know how you can keep so calm and normal when everyone's looking at us like we're animals in a zoo."

Kai glanced around at our sea of onlookers. "I guess I'm just used to it."

He said it with no hint of arrogance, simply stating a fact.

"We're going to set the Click rumor mill into overdrive again," I joked weakly.

Kai shook his head. "I'm so sorry about all those blasts after the dance."

"Not your fault."

Freaking, stupid, obnoxious Click.

When we'd returned from GameON in Denver, our phones were waiting for us — ticking time bombs that would inevitably explode. We'd opened the Click blasts together, preparing for the worst. And they'd delivered.

First, Click again accused me of rigging the prom queen

nominations. This time, though, it insinuated that I'd done it in a desperate attempt to get close to the popular kids.

Which was, of course, ridiculous.

The next Click blast was a photo of us leaving the dance, along with the allegation that we had snuck out in shame because I'd realized I could never beat Madison Albright for prom queen.

Not too terrible.

But the third one had been the worst. It said that Kai had asked me to the dance as a joke, to make fun of my Anti Prom Queen campaign. Which, as Kai had pointed out, was stupid, seeing as the Anti Prom Queen campaign had been his idea in the first place.

But, it still didn't feel good. And now, we were holding hands in public and eating lunch together. I wasn't exactly excited to see what Click was going to say about me next.

Kai must have noticed my frown, because he covered my hand with his. Squeezed it.

"Mac?"

"Yeah?"

"Do you trust me?"

I hesitated for a beat. Looked into those dark eyes and saw the boy behind them.

"Yes," I whispered softly.

"Then let's give them something to talk about." Kai smiled. Before I knew what was happening, he was standing on the table, clinking a spoon against his glass like he was about to give a speech at a wedding.

"Attention, Evermore High! Attention!" Heads turned. People held up their phones. Someone wolf-whistled. There were chuckles of nervous anticipation.

"For those of you who don't know me, my name is Kai Taylor. I'm on the basketball team. And in a few weeks, our team is going to win the state finals."

A huge, roaring cheer went up around the cafeteria. The basketball team leaped to their feet, exploding in whoops and yells.

"And as a future state final winner, I thought it was only fitting that I take a winner to the prom as my date." Kai grinned, the cat that got the cream. "A prom queen winner, to be exact."

The cheers grew louder.

All the breath left my lungs. What in heaven's name was he pulling?

Kai got down on one knee on the table.

What are you doing?" I hissed under my breath.

"Something I should have done ages ago." Kai stared into my eyes and I flushed under his gaze. He extended a hand to me. "Mackayla Lafelle, will you go to prom with me?"

For a moment, the entire cafeteria was silent, save for the deafening thud of my heart. My entire head was glowing bright red to match my hair.

"Y-yes," I squeaked.

"WOOOOO!" I vaguely registered Sofia jumping up and down a few tables away. Girls sighed at the romance of it all. Boys catcalled and howled.

Kai jumped off the table and kissed me right on the lips in front of everyone. He put his mouth close to my ear. "I really like you, Mac. Like, a lot."

A thrill ran down my spine. "I really like you, too, Kai Taylor."

Then, our moment was abruptly cut short as the lunch-room supervisor reached us. He pulled Kai away by the arm. "Cute stunt, Mr. Taylor. Have two days of detention for your troubles."

Kai flashed me a grin. "It was worth it."

I couldn't keep the smile off my face if I tried, my eyes locked on Kai's. He received a standing ovation from the student body as he was escorted from the cafeteria. He laughed as he went, grinning from ear to ear.

Kai freaking Taylor had asked me to prom! And he'd asked me in the most public way possible, not caring what Click would have to say about it. Or that he'd be writing lines after school as punishment for his stunt.

I looked around the room, revelling in the moment... and then my eyes landed on a cold, green-eyed stare.

One person wasn't joining in the applause.

Madison.

2 4

KAI

*T*wo weeks of kissing Mackayla Lafelle and I was on top of the world.

In school, we held hands and ate lunch together. It became easier and easier to ignore the stares and whispers that came from all directions. And miraculously, that shut Click up for a little while.

Mac even came to my basketball games, sitting in the front row and wearing my Panthers hoodie with my name and number on the back. And, I went to her house after school as often as my parents allowed me to. I watched Shaun make art out of his food at dinner, before Mac and I worked on our VGP homework together and played video games until curfew.

I was actually getting pretty good at Mall Zombies, much to Mac's chagrin.

Tonight, my parents were gone, so I'd challenged Mac and Shaun to a pickup game in my driveway. Lafelle Siblings vs. Taylor.

It was down to the final moments. I edged closer to Mac, enjoying the excuse to get near to her under the guise of defense. She looked adorable, all bundled up in a hat and scarf to protect against the chilly, early spring evening air. She neatly hopped up on the curb, out of my reach, and took a left-handed shot.

The ball spun awkwardly in the air, smashed against the backboard, and somehow, by some miracle, made it in the hoop.

Mac cheered, jumping up and down. She held her fists in the air in a victory stance. "MVP! MVP!"

"Not so fast." I laughed. "That was totally out of bounds."

"Says who?" Mac demanded, doing a little victory dance. "I say it counts. 20 all."

Her face was flushed, her eyes glittering. I wanted to grab her and kiss her. But Shaun was present, so I settled for tickling her ribs instead. She shrieked, ducking away from me.

"20 - 20," Shaun said seriously, observing us with solemn eyes.

"You're the boss." I tipped my imaginary cap to him, then threw him the ball. "Next basket wins."

Shaun dribbled the ball clumsily towards me. He narrowed his eyes, and poked his tongue out of the side of his mouth, deep in concentration. I half-heartedly held my hands up, trying to appear like I was defending when, in reality, all I wanted was for him to make the winning shot.

Shaun ducked left, and I made a show of tripping over my feet, letting him get past me. He threw his little arms up in the air, chucking the ball with all his might... and it went in!

"Yeahhhh!" A lion's roar ripped out of my mouth. I dived towards Shaun, picking him up and swinging him onto my shoulders. He clenched his gloved fists together, cheering at the top of his lungs.

"I did it! I did it! Mac, did you see that? I beat Kai Taylor!" Shaun squealed.

Mac was watching Shaun and I, her eyes sparkling. "I did see that. Amazing shot."

I reached up and lifted Shaun off my shoulders. I set him down gently on the ground.

"I gotta go tell Mom!" He went flying up the Lafelle's driveway like a tornado, cheering the whole way.

Mac ran to me and wrapped her arms around my neck. Kissed me hard on the mouth. "You are amazing. I don't think you understand how much this means to Shaun."

I brushed a lock of red hair from Mac's shining face. "I don't think you understand how much this means to *me*. Your family is the best."

I meant every word. Mac and Shaun brought so much joy and happiness and warmth into my world. Spending time with them and their mom was a true gift. They were such a tight, loving family unit — something I'd never experienced before.

Mac laughed and tossed the basketball in the air. Caught it. "Clearly we're the best at basketball, as we obviously beat you."

"You think?" I lowered my voice to a playful growl. "Is that a challenge, Mackayla?"

She smirked wickedly, her chest puffed out. She dribbled the ball, moving so that her back was practically against my chest. I circled her waist with my arms.

"Foul!" she shouted.

I hugged her closer to me.

"Sorry, I don't see a ref," I muttered into her ear.

She turned her head around, moving to kiss me. Distracted, I immediately forgot about the game, and leaned towards her. She seized my moment of weakness ruthlessly, wriggling out of my grip and dribbling the ball forward. She arced it into the net.

"Two to nothing!" Mac threw her arms in the air and twirled.

My lips tugged upwards at the corners. "Cheater."

"I say you cheated first." Mac grinned. She tossed me the ball, then used everything in her power to distract me as I moved it forward, hanging off my neck and tugging at my jacket.

"I thought you were good at this, Taylor," she crowed as she knocked the ball out of my hands.

"You might be the one person on earth I'm happy to lose to." This time, I couldn't wait any longer. I strode over to her, took her in my arms, and kissed her like I'd been wanting to all night.

After we were done with our 1-on-1 basketball game — which had quickly unraveled into little more than one massive makeout sesh — we sat on my front doorstep and shared a Gatorade. Mac leaned against me and I put my arm around her, keeping the cold away.

"How are you finding VGP class now?"

"Fine." I shrugged. "I'm grateful for everything you've taught me. I just got to make sure the next project I turn in passes so I can keep playing ball. Playoffs start soon, I can't slip up again."

"You won't." Mac sounded more confident than I felt. "Campaign day for the prom queen nominees is coming up next week already."

"We've totally been neglecting your campaign lately. I'm sorry," I replied. It was true. When Mac and I were together these days, the last thing we wanted to talk about was Evermore High or Click.

"Not your fault." Mac snuggled into my shoulder. "We'll think of something."

"I'm sure whatever we think of, Click will crucify you for it."

Mac sat up with a start, knocking the Gatorade bottle over in the process. Neon yellow liquid seeped over the step and dripped off the edge. "That's it!"

"What's it?" I frowned, picking up the now-empty bottle and screwing the cap on.

Mac was practically bouncing up and down with happiness. "I know what we need to do for Campaign Day."

2 5

MAC

I hopped from foot to foot, dizzy with anticipation. Around me, my squad of helpers were in their places, all wearing T-shirts emblazoned with "Vote for the Anti Prom Queen." Across the gym, Madison was standing at the front of her pack of cheerleaders, glowering at our display.

I didn't think I'd ever been so nervous in my life.

After we'd enlisted the help we needed, it had still taken the better part of a week to put together my Campaign Day presentation. Kai, Sofia, Noah, and I had then spent hours setting it all up in the school gym last night.

And in just a few short minutes, the rest of the school would see it, too.

Next to me, Kai squeezed my hand. "You got this, Mac."

I gave him a little smile. The gym doors opened and the flood of students poured in.

I held my breath.

Our Campaign Day approach had been risky. With the blessing of everyone involved, Kai and I had created dioramas of the biggest moments Click had targeted

123

students. We had dioramas of Chase Jones being falsely accused of cheating to sabotage his relationships, Hailey Danielson being horrifically, wrongly shamed after Adam Zamos broke up with her and she started seeing Trey, Jordyn Jones's every move being tracked by Click for an entire summer for sport. We also had dioramas of Noah Lyons hiding from the Click paparazzi all of last semester. And me, in all my gross, sweaty glory, sniffing my own armpits.

We'd stuck up posters around the dioramas, saying things like "Evermore, we are better than this" and "Let's build each other up, not tear each other down." And the people featured in the dioramas were stationed in front of them, ready to talk to passersby about their experiences being hassled by Click.

As the Evermore students began to look around, Jordyn produced a bullhorn from goodness-knows-where, and started yelling for people to come look at our display.

"A vote for Mac is a vote against Click!" she yelled, stalking back and forth like a circus ringmaster, chest puffed out.

Her approach was working.

I watched as Chase hugged a freshman girl who'd been harassed on Click for her dating life. Hailey was telling a sophomore who'd been ridiculed for her outfit choices to be proud of who she was. And Dylan was high-fiving a student athlete who'd been grilled on Click about his sexuality.

Abby and Sofia circled the crowd, passing out flyers that asked "Could this be the end of Click's reign of destruction?"

In the middle of the display, we'd hung a gigantic, blank poster asking people to share their experiences of feeling victimized or bullied by Click. Multiple students were grabbing markers and writing things down. Others were taking selfies in front of the board.

Our risk was paying off. People were getting into this.

"Don't look now, but someone is royally pissed," Kai murmured in my ear.

I, of course, immediately jerked my head to look. Across the gym, Madison — flanked by Becca and Lauren — was glaring daggers at us. When my eyes met Madi's, she gave her head a little shake.

I rolled my eyes in response. I was sick of Madison Albright and her cronies thinking they owned the school because they were beautiful and popular, and for now, Click was on their side.

Fuelled by annoyance, I marched up to Jordyn.

"Can I borrow that?" I pointed at her bullhorn.

"Sure!" She flung it in my direction and shook her hair. Her cheeks were red and she was breathing heavily. "I was getting a little hopped up on power, anyhow. Use it wisely."

Before I could think about what I was doing and chicken out, I climbed up on a table.

"Hello!" I said into the horn, and then almost fell over in shock at the sound of my voice booming around the gym. A few people stopped and stared, raising their eyebrows expectantly. I took a deep, shaky breath, and continued.

"My name is Mackayla Lafelle, and I'm running as Anti Prom Queen. A vote for me is a vote for anyone who's had enough of being bullied or intimidated for looking, or dressing, or acting different." I glanced around the room, nodding at students who were staring up at me. "A vote for me is a vote for anyone who's felt victimized by Click and the poisonous rumors and lies it spreads. A vote for me is a vote for ending Click and treating everyone with respect! A vote for me is—"

"Miss Lafelle, please get down from that table immediately." Mr. Adebayo's booming voice cut me off.

I looked at the teacher, who was standing right beneath me, arms folded across his chest.

Oops.

I dropped the bullhorn and scrambled to the ground. "Sorry, I, uh — got a bit carried away."

"I see that," Mr. Adebayo said. "And, loathe as I am to stop anyone from an impassioned speech, unfortunately, this was a health and safety ruling. No students on folding tables and all that. Just doing my job."

He smiled at me. Wait... was I not in trouble?

"But, as far as I can tell, all looks in order now." Mr. Adebayo winked. "Good luck, Mackayla. I hope you win."

And just like that, he was gone. I stared after him, open-mouthed.

Kai jogged up to my side. "Nice speech. You get detention for that stunt or what?"

A grin slowly spread across my face. "Nope. I think I got a faculty vote, actually."

Kai put his arms around me. "Only you, Mac. Only you."

Today was turning out to be a really good day.

I was still wrapped in Kai's arms when my phone vibrated in my pocket.

I pulled it out.

It was from Click. A private direct message, this time. Anonymous.

Kai peered over my shoulder. Sighed. "What do they want now?"

Nice work today. But, do you really think that's all it's gonna take? Click runs this school. And once Kai Taylor's dirty laundry is aired in the open for all to see, you aren't going to be able to keep this pathetic little act going any longer. Remember your place, Mackayla: bottom of the food chain. #MacvsClick

My heart sped up with every threatening word, and a sick feeling settled in my stomach.

I lifted my head and saw Madison glaring at me. The

same way she'd glared at me in the cafeteria when Kai had asked me to prom.

"Earth to Mackayla?" Kai's words jolted me back to reality. "You okay?"

"Yeah, I'm fine." I smiled tightly. "What do you think they mean?"

Kai scoffed. "Whatever it is, I don't care. Let those losers try what they want. They can't blackmail us."

"I don't want you to get publicly dragged through the mud because of me," I said.

Kai's phone buzzed.

As he read the message, his face fell.

"Click?" I said, craning my neck to take a look. But, before I could see his phone, he locked the screen and slipped it back in his pocket.

"Nah. Just Zane texting me," he said. But, his expression looked too frantic, his words too rushed.

"You okay?" I put my hand on his arm.

Kai smiled, shrugging my touch away. "Don't worry about me, Mac. Click can't hurt me. It's an empty threat."

MAC

"So, basically, I need to put in a command here for an if/then conditional statement?" Kai looked up from his laptop screen.

"You got it." I nodded. "You barely even need my help anymore."

Kai grinned from where he was sprawled across my bed. "Doubtful. You're saving me."

I rolled my eyes, my cheeks warm from a blush. But, despite Kai's humility, I knew I was right. The more we worked on projects for Video Game Production class, the less he needed me. He had the whole thing figured out. And, as I had long suspected, Kai Taylor wasn't half as dumb as everyone made him out to be.

I spun around in my desk chair and my eyes flickered back to my computer screen, where I was mocking up my own text RPG game. But, I couldn't concentrate.

It had been a few days since Click's threat on Campaign Day. And, though Kai insisted that he didn't care about Click and its threats, I could tell that something was off with him. I could see it in his eyes. He was keeping something from me.

"Hey, Kai?" I ventured. Nerves knotted in my stomach and my palms began to sweat.

He rolled over onto his front, and the corners of his mouth pulled upwards into a half-smile. "What's up?"

"The other day, what did Click mean by 'airing your dirty laundry?'" I asked tentatively, staring at my clasped fingers on my lap. "What do you think they have on you?"

Kai rubbed his index fingers across his temples and exhaled slowly. He looked like he was considering his next words carefully. "Probably just more stuff about me being stupid? Failing classes?"

I frowned. "That's hardly dirty laundry. Click called you out for failing VGP months ago."

"Well I don't know, Mackayla. It could be anything." His mouth set in a grim line, and he got to his feet abruptly, almost knocking his laptop to the floor. I hated seeing him upset like this.

Hated that, because of me, Click was threatening him. He acted like he didn't care, but he clearly did.

"Sorry, I didn't mean–"

"No, I'm sorry," he said, cutting me off. He ran his fingers through his hair, his expression soft and vulnerable. "I sounded like a jerk. I shouldn't let Click get to me."

"Kai, you don't have to continue helping me with this Anti Prom Queen thing," I said sincerely. "You've done so much already and I feel responsible for dragging you into this mess."

"No way." Kai folded his arms. "I'm not going to leave you to do this alone. We started this together and we'll end it together. Click will be powerless after we're done."

Kai held out his arms and I stepped into them, taking comfort in his warm embrace.

"It's going to be okay." His chest rumbled against my cheek as he spoke. It was incredibly soothing. "We just have to get this semester over with. I wish it was over already and we could go back to the way things used to be."

Kai's words tore me in a million directions.

I was still angry that someone had nominated me as prom queen as a joke, but I wouldn't change it now. The nomination had given me an opportunity to stand up to Click's bullying. And, inadvertently, it had brought Kai and I together. Changed him from my annoying, cocky neighbor into a boy who had bared his soul to me. A boy I had fallen for.

But what if that wasn't enough?

A sickening thought occurred to me. Kai was putting up walls with me again, keeping things from me all of a sudden... Like he was backing away from me.

So, when he said that he wanted to return to "the way things used to be"... When?

Did he mean that he wanted to go back to before Click was after him?

Or back to before we got together?

Goosebumps erupted on my skin. Kai's arms around me felt safe, reassuring. He was my anchor.

But his words left me untethered.

27

KAI

*M*y heart pounded loudly in my ears as I stepped out of Mackayla's house. I looked left, then right, then left again. Pulled my baseball cap low over my eyes.

I couldn't see anyone, so I made a dash for it.

I sprinted next door and slammed my front door shut behind me. My lungs heaved, but not from the run.

This was bad. Really bad.

Mac knew something was wrong.

She was asking me questions.

And, with every added hint of mistrust in her eyes, something inside me died a little more. I hated seeing it. I was hurting her. I was pushing her to feel like this.

But, there was nothing I could do about it. What could I tell her?

No way Click would stoop this low. No freaking way. Whoever was behind this was bluffing. Trying to scare me.

I couldn't take any chances, though. Not with what was on the line.

28

MAC

*M*y float for the Prom Court Parade was nothing short of spectacular.

In my opinion, at least.

The entire float was decked out with bunches of balloons and streamers, along with cutouts of our panther logo. All in black and silver, of course — Evermore High's school colors. In the middle of the float, there was a gigantic red sign with a line through it, symbolizing our stance against Click.

With just two days before the parade, Kai and I had arrived early at school and were working on the finishing touches: lettered flags spelled out *Mackayla Lafelle, the Anti Prom Queen Candidate.*

"Looking good," Kai said as he stuck a letter A flag in place. The other candidates had all used free periods to do their float work, but Kai insisted that we work on the float in the hours before school, or in the evenings, when nobody else was around.

I shivered in anticipation. "I hope everyone likes it."

Though the Prom Court Parade was not something I could

bring myself to look forward to, I could at least be proud of my float. I tried to ignore the fact that I'd be riding on, and therefore stuck in the center of attention for the whole town to see.

"They'll love it," Kai said. "How could they not?"

A quick glance around the deserted staff parking lot — where the floats were stored — did little to reassure me. Madison's float was a gorgeous, opulent display of purple and gold, decorated in crowns and sparkly jewels. It screamed royalty. Ben's float cleverly displayed a visual for all of the extracurriculars available at Evermore High. Chase and Dylan looked to have done a shared float, which was all-state champion football-themed, of course.

And Jordyn? Well, Jordyn Jones continued to support me — a relative stranger — more than I could've ever imagined. She'd refused to make a float, adamant that she wasn't campaigning. I was really beginning to like the girl.

"I don't know, I'm still super nervous." A thought suddenly occurred to me. "Hey, do you want to ride on my float with me? Keep me company?"

Kai's face clouded over as he processed my words. Not the reaction I'd been hoping for.

"You know," I backtracked wildly. "Just because you've been such a huge part of getting my campaign off the ground. Without you, I would've been way more of a laughingstock than I have been through this whole thing."

"Oh, I, uh..." Kai fumbled desperately. Embarrassment crept up my neck and into my cheeks, tinting my skin red.

There was a horribly awkward silence, but the truth was louder than ever. Kai didn't want to be seen with me on the float.

"Never mind," I said quickly, looking at the ground as my cheeks burned. "It was a stupid idea, anyway."

"No, Mac, it's not that." Kai's voice was strangely high-pitched, tinged with a note of desperation. "It's complicated, you see, because—"

"I get it," I interrupted, desperate for this awkwardness to be over. "Forget I asked."

Kai glowered at the ground before kicking a rock. Hard. It went skipping across the entire parking lot. We both watched it bounce away.

Then, he looked at me, his face stricken.

"Mackayla." He took a step towards me. "There's something I need to tell—"

"TAYLOR!" A deep voice boomed from behind us. Kai leaped backwards, away from me.

Did he not want to be seen with me? Was he embarrassed of me or something? Was that it?

It had never bothered him to be seen with me before. But ever since Click declared it was coming after him, it was like he'd had a personality transplant. Was he more worried about his alleged "dirty laundry" than he wanted to admit?

"Oh, hey Zane!" Kai called, taking another careful step away from me. "What's up?"

Zane Bridgers, one of Kai's teammates, walked towards us with a cocky grin on his face.

"Float looks... good." His tone was mocking and his expression clearly communicated he thought otherwise.

"Thanks?" I said. I waited for Kai to defend my float.

He didn't.

"What do you want, Zane?" Kai said instead.

"Been looking for you everywhere, dude. I texted you like 10 times. Big pep rally happening first period. Coach got the whole team together in the gym, but we're missing our big-shot superstar."

"Oh. My bad. Phone was on silent."

"Dummy." Zane punched Kai on the arm and grinned.

"Now, come on. Coach is going to kill us if we aren't there in two minutes."

Kai looked at me, his eyes wild. He chewed his lip for a moment.

Then, his face went blank. "Better go, then. Later, Mac."

"Later," I mumbled, watching Zane pull Kai in the direction of the gym. Watching the boy I was falling for walk away to take his place at the school's center stage — where he belonged as a star athlete.

Zane said something to Kai, and Kai laughed. The sound was warm, like sunshine.

Neither of them looked back.

29

KAI

"*H*ey Mac, what did you do for question 26?" I whispered.

Mac looked up from her laptop. "You know the answer to that."

I sighed.

I did know the answer. She'd taught me how to do this just last week. But she'd barely said hi to me when I came into VGP class, and she'd been staring at her computer screen ever since. Like she was trying to avoid eye contact.

I just wanted to make conversation, get her to talk to me. She'd been distant since we were decorating her float the other morning and Zane showed up. But I guess I didn't blame her.

"Have you thought of any game ideas for the ES Games competition?" I asked, my mind scrambling for topics of conversation. Mr. Vargas had given us the period to work on our last project of the semester — a more advanced RPG game — and he didn't seem to mind that, around the room, people were talking.

Mac shook her head. "I can't even think about that right now. I just need to get through all this prom crap first."

There was a beat of silence.

"Are you doing okay with everything?" I asked quietly.

"Course," she snapped. But she didn't look okay. Her face was pale, her hair scraped back in a haphazard braid. Instead of her usual black eyeliner, her eyes were ringed with dark circles that indicated she hadn't slept last night.

I worried that this was all my fault.

"Mac, I—"

Before I could get another word out, Mac swung around in her chair to face me. "You what, Taylor? What is it this time?"

The anger in her eyes stung me like a wasp.

"Nothing." I chickened out, turning back to my computer.

"Nothing?" Mac folded her arms across her chest. "Or is it that you're scared of Click tearing you off your popularity throne if you keep associating with me?"

Of course that was what she thought was happening. That was exactly how it looked.

"No," I said slowly.

"Hmm." Mac tapped her chin sarcastically. "Let me see. So, the only time you'll speak to me lately is in my room, or when nobody else is around. You avoid me at school. And you're choosing to talk to me now. In VGP class. When none of your friends are around. What, exactly, am I meant to think?"

Mac was trying to talk the tough game, but her voice cracked with hurt.

And it was my fault.

I winced. "It's not like that."

"It sure looks like it is."

I was at a complete loss. How could I tell her the truth? How could I tell her that Click was blackmailing me to stay away from her in public, and I was doing my best to comply? Not for my sake... but for hers?

No. She couldn't know that.

She'd want to face Click head-on, publicly. And she would end up even more hurt when everything unraveled.

I pasted a big, fake, cocky smile on my face. Leaned back in my chair. "Lighten up, MacLovin."

Shock streaked across Mac's face, quickly followed by profound sadness. She looked hurt, disappointed. Then, her expression went flat, neutral. Distant. I wasn't sure which was worse.

"It's *McLovin*, Taylor." Her voice was sharp and cold. "If you're going to go back to insulting nicknames, at least get them right."

And with that, she jumped to her feet and stormed from the room. I wanted to run after her, comfort her, tell her everything. But I couldn't.

It was better she thought I was the bad guy.

If that's what it took to protect her, then so be it.

30

MAC

*M*y sneakers squelched as I stepped in another puddle. It didn't matter, though — my shoes were full of water already. My hair was soaking wet, and the long, snaky strands were caked to my skull. I was sure my eyeliner was now a black river running down my cheeks.

After final period, I'd legged it out of school as quickly as possible. The last thing I wanted was to run into Kai on my way out. Today, I did NOT want a ride.

So much so that I'd walked home in the rain. Without an umbrella.

McLovin. UGH.

And I thought we'd come so far. Was I a complete idiot for thinking that Kai Taylor was different? For thinking that I'd been wrong about him? I couldn't even take solace in the fact that it was Friday because the stupid prom parade was tomorrow. Which meant I'd be seeing all of my favorite people from school anyway.

After what seemed like an eternity, I finally arrived home. I slowed to a stop as I approached our house, confused.

There was a white Lexus SUV parked in our driveway.

That wasn't Mom's and it certainly didn't belong to anyone I knew. Who was that? A friend of my mom's?

But she usually wasn't home this early.

I put my head down and stalked the last few feet to our house, slamming the front door behind me. I shook like a wet dog, sending a spray of water all over our entryway. I was sure Mom would be thrilled about that. I made a mental note to grab a towel and wipe up the mess later.

I stepped out of my sodden Vans and took off my jacket — fat lot of good it had done. Under it, my t-shirt was plastered to my body.

"Mom, whose Lexus is parked in our driveway?" I called.

No reply.

"Mom?"

"Mom's not here," Shaun shouted from the kitchen.

I padded towards the kitchen, removing my wet socks as I went. "Shaun, what are you—?"

I rounded the corner and stopped dead, my words dying on my tongue.

Madison Albright.

Correction: a stylishly dressed, flawlessly made-up, and completely bone-dry Madison Albright. Sitting in my kitchen. With my little brother.

"What in the?!"

Madison looked up and flashed me a faux-sympathetic smile. "Oh, Mackayla. Did you get a little wet on your way home?"

My jaw was on the floor. She reached for a hand towel hanging on the side of the island and passed it to me, like this was her house or something.

"What do you want, Madison?" I asked quietly.

"Oh, I was just having a very nice chat with your brother, here. Right, Shaun?"

Shaun's eyes were wide, like he wasn't sure.

Madison laughed. It was a rich, indulgent sound. "Your little brother is just the cutest."

Fear swirled in my stomach. "Shaun, upstairs."

"Why?" His little face crumpled. "What did I do?"

I felt terrible, but I needed to get him out of here. Stat. He was a tiny little fish, and Madison was a Great White shark, ready to feed.

Ignoring Madison's amused expression, I crouched to Shaun's level and took his hands. "You did nothing wrong, buddy, but I need to have a private conversation with Madison. So I want you to do me a big favor and go to your room for a little while. I'll come upstairs after and we'll play Mall Zombies. Deal?"

Shaun nodded solemnly. "Deal."

As soon as I heard his footsteps on the stairs, I turned my attention back to Madison. She was casually looking at her nails, her face perfectly bored and beautiful. She didn't even have a single hair out of place.

"What do you think you're doing, coming here?" I asked, my jaw tense.

Madison gestured to the stool beside her. "Please, sit."

I stayed standing.

"Fine, suit yourself." She waved one airy hand. "I came here to warn you about something."

I narrowed my eyes. "Warn me about what?"

"You need to quit the prom queen race. Now."

"No." I folded my arms, tilted my head and met her stare.

She laughed again. "Oh, Mackayla. One day, you'll see that I'm only trying to protect you."

I paused. Wavered. Then, perhaps against my better judgement, I took the bait. "What do you mean, protect me?"

"Let's just say that, if you don't pull out of the race, Click is going to get ugly at the prom parade tomorrow."

"Is that a threat, Madison?" I took a step towards her,

careful to keep my voice and movements calm and deliberate. I wouldn't let her see how much her words affected me. Wouldn't give her the satisfaction.

"Absolutely not." She held up both her hands. The universal symbol of surrender. "All I'm saying is, be careful who you trust. That little boyfriend of yours, for starters."

It was my turn to laugh. "Oh, you mean the one who turned you down at Hailey's party?"

I may have been mad at Kai, but I trusted him *way* more than I'd ever trust Madison. Even if he'd been acting weird lately, Madison was a snake.

Madison got to her feet. Picked up her purse and strung it over one shoulder. "All I'm saying, Mackayla, is that sometimes, people keep their friends close and their enemies closer. It's impossible to know who to trust. But I'm not the bad guy here. And when Click strikes again, don't say I didn't warn you."

"Why would I ever believe you?" I snapped.

Madison's glittering green eyes softened for a moment. "Because I'm your only competition. But, I came here to warn you."

With that, she strolled towards the front door, her stilettos clicking on the linoleum. She stopped in the entryway to snap open her designer umbrella.

"It's bad luck to open your umbrella inside," I said. Sure it was petty, but I couldn't help myself.

Madison looked at me pityingly. "Sweetie, I don't need luck, good or bad. But I do wish *you* nothing but good luck tomorrow."

And with that, she disappeared out the front door. I stared after her, slack-jawed.

What was all THAT about?

I decided that I didn't want to find out. Madison was right about one thing — she was the competition. The enemy. Tomorrow was important to my Anti Prom Queen campaign, and Madison was obviously just trying to psych me out.

Wasn't she?

My phone buzzed. Probably some stupid Click blast.

I didn't need this crap.

I turned off my phone, and ran up the stairs to Shaun.

31

KAI

"Tay-lor, Tay-lor!" My teammates chanted as I hopped on the bus.

I tried my best to smile as I walked down the aisle, high-fiving everyone as I went. But my heart wasn't in it.

"Awesome D tonight, Edgar," I said to a sophomore who was built like a tank. He'd had a couple of huge blocks tonight.

My teammate grinned big, glowing with the praise. "Couldn't have done it without you."

"It was a team effort," I murmured, dipping my eyes downward. Basketball was a team sport, and we'd all contributed to our semifinal win against Marymount High.

It had been a gruelling, physical and very close game. Marymount had played well and their home crowd had almost blown the roof off their gym. But, at the last second, on the buzzer, I'd thrown a three pointer that had flipped the game in our favor, and Evermore had come away with the victory and a place in tomorrow night's state finals.

After another round of high-fives and congratulations, I flopped down in the empty seat beside Zane, exhausted. I flipped the lid open on my water bottle and guzzled the contents. We had a two-hour bus ride home, and I planned on napping for the entire length of the journey.

"You were on fire out there tonight," Zane said.

I nodded at him. "You too. I saw your parents in the stands."

Zane laughed. "Yeah, good old Mom and Dad cheering me on, as usual. Would've swapped them out for a couple hot senior girls yelling for me, wouldn't you?"

"I wouldn't know," I said crisply, closing my eyes. My own parents had, of course, not bothered to make the drive to Marymount. Dad had texted me after the game to ask for a report of how many points I'd put up and how many assists I'd made.

I hadn't replied.

Zane laughed, mistaking the source of my annoyance. "Oh, I forgot. You're in love with Mackayla Lafelle now. You have no care for hot senior girls."

My eyes snapped open. "Shhh."

"Where was she tonight, Taylor? Weird girl didn't want to enjoy her moment of fame dating our winning scorer?"

"Shut up, Zane," I said between gritted teeth. I'd texted Mackayla after school to check if she was coming. She hadn't replied. Hadn't shown up.

With what Click was threatening, I knew it was for the best. But it still stung.

Zane poked me in the ribs. "Oooh, touchy about our new girlfriend, are we?"

"No." I glanced around to see if anyone was listening. Luckily, the rest of the team seemed distracted. They were singing along to a new rap song that was blaring from the bus's old speakers.

He cocked an eyebrow at me. "So, it is true?"

"What?" I hissed.

"I didn't believe it at first." Zane shook his head, his eyes shining in wonder. "I actually thought you'd fallen for her. Didn't understand why. But I should've known better. You absolute legend!"

He punched me in the arm and I stared at him in bewilderment. "What are you talking about?"

"It was your idea to nominate Mac for prom queen as a joke, right?" Zane laughed. "You always had that little neighbor rivalry going, but you really kicked it up a notch. Getting her nominated instead of Hailey? Brilliant prank. And then, you even pretended to date her to keep the joke going, get her to actually campaign for the thing."

I stared at him with my mouth open. What on earth was he talking about?

Oblivious to my confusion, Zane held his hand up for a high five. "Le-gen-dary, bro."

"What, I… no…" I felt dizzy all of a sudden, like all the blood was draining from my face. I swatted Zane's hand away. "Is that what everyone thinks?"

Zane wasn't listening. "Bro, you even had *me* fooled for a while. Nice work. This may be the best prank the school has ever seen."

The world was swimming around me, blurry and out of focus. "But it wasn't me."

My stomach twisted into a horrible knot as realization hit. Was this the work of Click? I'd been pushing Mackayla away, thanks to its blackmail. But what if I'd played right into its hands?

This was cruel, uncalled for, and completely hurtful. Which fit with Click's MO. Worried for the girl I'd fallen hopelessly in love with, I was pulling back. In the meantime, Click had been getting ready to blindside me with a totally different rumor: That this whole thing – our whole relationship – had been a joke to me.

And, thanks to my own actions, I looked guilty as sin.

My phone buzzed in my lap and a chill went down my spine.

"She said it was," Zane said, but I wasn't listening.

"Hmm?" I said noncommittally as I checked my phone. Click had sent me a message.

What did it have to say now?

I opened the blast.

And immediately panicked.

Zane and my teammates faded into oblivion as I stared at the anonymous private message. There was a photo in the blast that told me Click wasn't messing around. Whoever was blackmailing me was very, very serious.

The text attached was just as bad: *Stay away from that ginger freak. Don't speak to her or look at her in public. And ditch her as your prom date. Or else, tomorrow's prom parade will reveal something you don't want to see.*

The world lurched sideways and I looked at my watch. 11pm. We wouldn't be home until well after midnight.

My heart hammered in my chest. What would Click's next move be?

I fired off a quick text to Mac: *SOS - need to speak to you before the prom parade tomorrow. Urgent.*

I stared at my phone, willing it to beep with a response. But, none came.

All I could do was hope I wasn't too late.

MAC

ap-tap-tap.

I rolled over in bed, feeling groggy and disoriented. I checked the alarm clock on my nightstand.

It was 8am. On a Saturday morning. Nobody should be awake at this hour.

And what on earth was making that noise?

Tap-tap-tap.

It was coming from… ah, the window.

"What does he want?" I grumbled, throwing the covers off my bed and clambering to my feet.

I went to the window. Rays of morning sunshine sliced through the slats in the blinds, deeming the soggy showers of yesterday to be a distant memory. So much for hoping the prom parade would get rained out.

I opened my blinds and threw open the window. Realized too late that my hair was in a crazy bird's nest of tangles and I was wearing Minecraft pajamas. I swallowed my embarrassment and glared across the way at my branch-wielding neighbor.

"What, Taylor?" I put on the snappiest voice I could muster. "You woke me up."

Kai peered out his window, seemingly not even noticing my bedraggled appearance. He looked pale and tired, like he hadn't slept a wink. His hair was messy and unkempt and his cheeks were hollow. "Mac, why aren't you texting me back?"

"Didn't get your texts." I shrugged, crossing my arms. "Turned my phone off."

Kai's face contorted. He bit his lip uneasily, and he was jiggling the branch he'd just used to scratch my window back and forth frantically. Something was very off.

"What's going on?" I asked, my voice a touch softer.

"Mac, I am so, so sorry about yesterday. But, I need to talk to you, explain something to you. Just…" He locked eyes with me. Ran his fingers through his hair. "Just wait there, okay? I'm coming over to talk to you."

Before I could respond, Kai bolted, disappearing out his bedroom door.

What just happened? What did Kai want to talk to me about?

I decided I might as well make myself somewhat presentable. I quickly threw my hair into a ponytail and gurgled some mouthwash to freshen my breath.

Ding dong!

"I'll get it." I scrambled down the stairs and ran for the front door. Flung it open. "What's going on?"

"Uhh… I'm here to help you get ready?"

Instead of Kai, Sofia stood on my doorstep. She was carrying a huge makeup case in one hand, and an assortment of shoes in the other. She looked at me quizzically, an eyebrow raised.

"Oh, Sof, sorry. I thought you were someone else." I held open the door to allow my best friend to come into the house.

Just as a breathless Kai Taylor appeared in my driveway. His hair was in disarray and he was wearing his grey sweats. His eyes were wide and frantic. "Mac, I—"

He stopped dead when he saw Sofia. He opened and closed his mouth, looking like a deer in the headlights.

"Sofia's here to help me get ready." I stated the obvious. "What's up?"

Kai looked from me to Sofia and back again. "Uh, um. Nothing. Maybe we can talk later?"

I nodded jerkily, biting back my frustration. First, he avoids me like the plague, then he inundates me with texts and wakes me up, desperate to talk to me? What was his deal right now?

But, I supposed it would have to wait until after the parade. After all, he was the one who'd refused to ride in the float with me... what could he possibly want that was so urgent?

"I'll find you after the parade," I promised.

Instead of replying, he stared at me blankly. Man, he was acting weird.

I tilted my head. "You okay?"

He swallowed, then nodded. "Good luck today, Mac."

The way he said it suggested I would need it. Despite the warm morning sunshine, I shivered.

MAC

*E*verything had been going so well.

At home, Sofia helped me do my makeup and fix my hair. I donned the outfit we'd picked out together – a black T-shirt with "Vote for Mac" in silver writing across the front, a black jean skirt that was form fitting but classic, and black tights. Oh, and my purple Doc Martens for a splash of color.

We'd driven over to school together, singing along to the Luminous at the highest level. I'd hoped it would dispel some of the nervous energy in my body. It didn't.

And then, we'd arrived in the staff parking lot and my already uneasy stomach twisted further. Yesterday's rainfall had wreaked havoc on most of Evermore, and though the floats had been parked under a carport, the shelter hadn't been a match for the monsoon-like downpours.

My float had been parked at the edge. Meaning it took the brunt of the damage.

Sofia and I approached slowly, like we were approaching a swarm of bees. My heart sank with each step closer to the mess that had once been my float. The paper streamers formed a soggy clump, and the ink on my signs had bled everywhere.

Sofia clapped her hands over her mouth and looked at me, her eyes like saucers. "Mac, I'm so sorry…"

"What am I going to do?" I moaned, poking at the clump of streamers.

"Is there anything I can do to help?"

A cool hand landed on my shoulder, and I turned to see Hailey standing next to me. She was dressed in her cheerleading uniform, silver ribbons in her gold hair. Her eyes were wide and worried, and her mouth was twisted into a disappointment grimace.

I shook my head, determined to keep my tears at bay. "Thanks, Hailey, but I don't think so. It's kind of ruined."

Hailey gave me a sympathetic smile. "If it's any consolation, I think you still have a great chance at winning."

"Agreed!" Jordyn bounded up, skidding to a halt next to her best friend. "If anything, the wet signs just add to the look."

"Chaos," Abby added, appearing out of nowhere. "I can write an article for the Pinnacle saying you intended this sort of gloomy, morose look to symbolize the chaos Click causes."

I stared at the three senior girls, stunned by their positivity and support. "What did I do to deserve you all?"

"You did what none of us were able to pull off." Jordyn grinned. "You went for Click's jugular."

Her compliment meant so much and I felt grateful for their kindness. I smiled at the ground, touched. "Thanks, guys."

Sofia, Jordyn, Hailey, Abby and I tried to salvage what we could. But, before I knew it, it was action time. Coach Garcia blew her whistle, and the parade assembled.

The Prom Court Parade typically started here at Evermore High before running the same route it did every year.

The school marching band always went first, resplendent in their black uniforms with shiny silver tassels. Then, the cheerleading squad followed, waving their pom-poms and dancing. Third, there was the football team, dressed in their letterman jackets and marching behind a "State Championship Winners" banner.

The basketball team followed them. From my position next to my damaged float, I spotted Kai easily. He was wrapped in an MVP flag and he looked… well, furious. Zane clapped him on the back and he glared in response, swatting his friend away.

What was going on with him today? I couldn't seem to figure him out.

But, this morning, he did mention he'd texted me. Curious, I took out my phone and powered it back on.

I had six missed calls and nine texts from him overnight.

I was about to open his first message when we were called to mount our floats. My stomach flipping, I shoved my phone into my pocket and hopped on my float. The announcer's float went first and Abby stood tall, her microphone in hand. She was MC-ing the parade.

After Abby, the rest of the prom court nominees followed suit. Chase and Dylan went first, followed by Ben, and then Madison. Fittingly, I brought up the rear. As the procession made its way out of the front gates of Evermore High, I did my best to smile and wave at the crowds gathered around the school.

Slowly but surely, our procession moved towards Main Street – where the main events would take place. In front of the town of Evermore.

Miserable, I watched as the movement of my float caused the soggy streamers to fall in clumps. They littered my float's wake with sad, wet strips of black and silver. Behind me, my "Anti Click" sign came loose and fell to the floor.

It was a disaster. But I did my best to keep smiling and waving. It was all I could do.

We finally — *finally* — came to a stop in the middle of Main Street. The crowd here was the thickest it had been, but I spotted my mom among the onlookers. Shaun was on her shoulders, giggling and waving... at Kai. Not me.

Of course.

Abby, in her best quiz-show-announcer voice, addressed the crowd. "Goooooooood afternoon, Evermore!"

A cheer went up. Abby went on to introduce the prom court nominees one by one. The crowd hollered and cheered as Chase and Dylan made a show of strolling across their float. They "ooh"d and "ahh"d as Ben demonstrated his. They laughed as Abby pointed to Jordyn, sitting on the floor next to her, and they whooped as Madison curtseyed for them.

My knees shook as I waited for my turn.

"And last, but not least," Abby announced. "Mackayla Lafelle!"

She beamed in my direction, and I waved for the crowd. Some people cheered. Others watched me in amusement. Thankfully, nobody booed.

Buzz!

My phone went off in my pocket.

Not now. I was barely surviving this parade as it was. I didn't need a distraction.

Buzz! Buzz! Buzz!

Across the crowd, students reached for their phones. Ahead in the procession, cheerleaders and athletes were doing the same.

Must be a Click blast.

"Mackayla is a junior at Evermore High and a straight-A student," Abby continued through the obvious distraction of the crowd. "Her hobbies include coding and..."

But even I tuned Abby out as the hush of whispers traveled across the crowd. People whispered behind their hands. There were stifled laughs. They pointed.

At me.

A group of sophomore girls at the front of the crowd were chattering frantically and snapping pictures of me. Their eyes were hungry and curious.

I glanced around the parade and a number of students were openly laughing as they looked at me. My heart hit the concrete and I looked at Jordyn. She checked her phone and then her eyes met mine. She was white as a ghost. Chase was looking at me sympathetically and Hailey was shaking her head.

I had no choice. I had to check.

I fumbled for my phone in my pocket. What had Click said now?

My fingers trembling, I opened the blast. There was a video at the top of the message, with a paragraph of text underneath. The video appeared to show a few members of the basketball team.

I skipped the video and went straight to the text.

This just in, Evermore. Turns out that Mackayla Lafelle didn't rig the ballot after all. The basketball team nominated her as a prank – and it was all Kai Taylor's idea. He even took it one step further, and got close to her to convince her to actually *run for queen to keep the prank going. It worked! Kudos, Kai. Guess our all-star's not as dumb as he looks.*

The world spun around me, a blurred mess of cruel laughter and jeering and taunts. A wave of nausea washed through my stomach and I felt like I might fall over. Flashes went off as people photographed my humiliation.

It was as public – and as degrading – as it could have been.

A perfectly planned attack.

Surely, surely, Kai wouldn't stoop so low as to do this to me?

I tried to focus as I looked around. Tried to ignore the sneers and jeers of my classmates. Finally, my gaze came to rest on Kai's face.

He was staring at me, his eyes wide in horror.

The look on his face told me that I didn't need to watch the video to get my answer.

I looked away. I felt like I was going to be sick.

From the float next to mine, Madison was looking at me. Her eyes were soft, rather than triumphant, as I might've expected. "Mackayla—"

"You were right," I cut her off. "Thanks for trying to warn me."

And then, I hopped off my float and I ran.

And ran.

And kept running until I was far, far away from the prom parade crowds.

Far away from Kai Taylor.

34

MAC

I turned off my phone, closed my blinds, and locked my bedroom door. Then, I sat down and tended to the blisters I'd gotten from running the entire three miles home at top speed while wearing Doc Martens.

One of the blisters had popped. I swapped a wet cotton ball over the raw wound, and inhaled sharply at the sensation. If I could concentrate on the physical pain – focus on the sting of antiseptic lotion sizzling against skinned flesh – then maybe, just for a moment, I could forget that my heart had been scooped out and trampled on for the entire town to see.

I pressed the cotton ball onto the blister harder. But, the sting subsided all too quickly, and my tears began to flow.

Tap-tap-tap.

The familiar sound of a branch brushing my window came repeatedly and urgently. I ignored it.

I'd been such an idiot, trusting Kai Taylor. Believing someone like him could like someone like me. I'd let him in to all the most vulnerable parts of my life — and he'd seemed so genuine when he'd hung out with Shaun, when he'd encouraged me to sign up for the ES Games competition, when he'd sought me out in the crowd at his basketball games so we could share a secret smile.

And it had all been a game, a big joke. A prank. A bet.

A deliberate attempt to humiliate me as gravely as possible.

No wonder he'd been pulling away from me lately, putting distance between us. He was passing VGP class now, and he'd successfully gotten me to participate in every prom court event. And I'd been stupid enough to believe that Kai Taylor was more than just a dumb, mean, popularity-hungry jock.

Even Madison had tried to warn me.

"Mac?" A small, timid voice called from the other side of my door. When had my family gotten home? How long had I been crying for?

I sniffed back my tears. "Hey, Shaun." I tried, and failed, to keep my voice level. "What's up, buddy?"

"Kai Taylor is here to see you."

"Tell him I'm not here," I said.

"But you are here," Shaun answered. He was the wrong person to ask to lie. He just didn't get it.

"Tell him I don't want to see him, then."

"But he's my friend?"

Shaun's words cracked my heart a little further. He truly loved Kai. My blood boiled at the thought of Kai laughing at Shaun behind his back. How dare he get close to my family as part of his sick prank.

"Please, Shaun. Just do as I ask," I pleaded.

Thankfully, Mom came to the rescue. "Shaun, Mac's not feeling well. Can you tell Kai she can't come to the door because she isn't feeling well?"

There was a heavy sigh and then footsteps banged down

the stairs. Shaun was apparently satisfied with that explanation.

"Can I come in, honey?" Mom asked gently.

"No," I moaned.

"Come on, Mac. Open up."

I picked myself up off the floor long enough to unlock my door. Mom came into my room and sat on my bed. She didn't demand an explanation, or ask me any questions. She just held out her arms.

And I collapsed into them. Mom stroked my hair and held me as I cried until my eyes were red and raw.

35

KAI

*S*aturday night. The state finals. We'd fought hard to get here.

It was everything I used to dream of.

But, standing center court, hand over heart for the National Anthem, I just wanted to go home.

For once in my life, basketball wasn't at the forefront of my mind. And the person who was occupying all of my brainspace believed that I had tricked her. That I had pretended to like her in order to publicly shame her. And now, she hated me.

Not that I blamed her.

As the school choir sang the closing lines of the Star Spangled Banner, I automatically scanned the packed gym for a shock of familiar red hair. But, my search came up empty.

Of course she wasn't here.

Beside me, Zane was standing tall, his chest puffed out. The very sight of him made me furious. Was he in on the lie? He caught me glaring and shot me a cocky smile. He was confident we would win tonight. That the legend that was Kai Taylor would take our team to victory.

Team MVP *and* prankster of the year. What an honor.

I felt like I was going to throw up. I'd gone straight from the disastrous prom parade to Mac's house. I had to try and tell her the blast was a lie. That things weren't as they seemed. But, she wouldn't see me.

Then, my dad came raging into my room and ordered me to get ready. I was almost late for the game, and so I hadn't even had the chance to confront my teammates about that crazy video blast.

Why had they all thought it was my idea?

The anthem ended and the marching band launched into a rousing chorus. The cheerleaders formed a pyramid and I watched blankly as Madison smiled wide for the crowd from the top tier. She was a shoo-in for the crown now that Mac had been taken care of.

Madi saw me watching and gave me a theatrical wink. Meanwhile, Hailey, next to her on the pyramid, glared at me. My stomach lurched. Hailey had always been nice to me, but she was obviously disgusted at the recent revelation that I was a liar, a cheater and a user.

It was somewhat reassuring that not everybody at this school hero-worshipped such horrible behavior.

The truth was that I didn't really care if some people hated me. Nobody had ever liked me for who I was anyway. I just wished I could tell Mac the truth. The thought of no longer having her in my life was painful. Her cheeky grin, her quick wit, our effortless banter.

It was killing me that I was causing her pain. But, Click had been clear in its threats, and I'd played right into its hands. Everyone thought I was guilty. And, if I tried to prove otherwise, Click would hurt her all the more.

See, I believed Click's threats now. Whoever was behind this would stop at nothing to get what they wanted.

The ref blew his whistle and the game began. I played on autopilot, going through the motions seamlessly. To an observer, I would've looked like I was at the top of my game. But inside, I was a mess.

At halftime, we were down by six. Back in the locker room, Coach launched into another pep talk, but I grabbed my phone.

One new message. My heart jolted.

I clicked on it.

And my heart sank like a stone.

Dad: *Get your head in the game, Kai. You shouldn't have missed that last three pointer, you were wide open. How's an easy miss like that going to look to any college scouts watching?*

My father was being his usual, charming self. No mention of the 19 points I had scored. Clearly, Dad bothered to show up to tonight's game for the sole purpose of berating me.

Coach blew his whistle and I snapped back to attention. We jogged back out to the court and I put my head down for the second half. It was rough and physical, and I threw myself into it with everything I had. In what seemed like the far distance, the crowd yelled and cheered, but the sound faded into oblivion. It was just me and the ball.

When the final whistle blew, we were up by eight.

I stood still at center court as the bench, the coaches, the cheer team all rushed onto the court. Everyone hugged, screamed, jumped up and down. My teammates piled on me. Threw their arms around me. Clapped my back. High-fived.

Coach McMorris put his big hands on my shoulders. His eyes were glistening. "I knew you had it in you, Taylor."

Coach kept a hand on my shoulder as the trophies were given out. I won MVP.

Following the winner's presentation, my dad made his

way onto the court. He wasn't smiling, but he also wasn't wearing that special scowl he seemed to reserve exclusively for me. He looked almost... proud. If circumstances were different, I would've been thrilled to see that unfamiliar look on his face.

But I felt nothing. Absolutely nothing.

My dream had come true. And all I wanted was to wake up and for it not to be real.

36

KAI

"*A* toast!" Zane cried, holding his red Solo cup high in the air. Around the yard, everyone copied his action. "To being the Colorado State Division 1 Champions!"

Cheers erupted. Cups clinked. Cheap beer sloshed.

I ignored it all. Sat down on a lawn chair and took a sip of water. Checked my phone again.

Nothing.

A victory party in Rob Altman's backyard was the last place I wanted to be, but I hadn't exactly been given a choice about my attendance by my teammates.

There were about a hundred people crammed into the yard — mostly athletes and cheerleaders. A bunch of people were in the hot tub. A cluster of guys manned the barbecue, flipping burgers and trying to look manly. Others were hanging out by the pool. Chase and Abby were in the middle of the group, kissing like nobody was around for miles. Nearby, Hailey and Jordyn were playing volleyball against Trey and Dylan. And beating them, too. The sight almost brought a smile to my face.

Almost.

"Chug! Chug! Chug!" Beside me, a bunch of guys started a drinking game, shoving each other and joking around.

But I walked away. I couldn't bring myself to be in a festive mood.

Then, I spotted Mac's friend Sofia and her boyfriend, Noah. They were sitting on the back porch swing together. I'd spent some time with the two of them over the months that Mac and I had been together. Noah, in particular, was a pretty cool guy. For having a super famous dad, he was incredibly humble. And funny. Sofia was just a bundle of energy and I could see how she and Mac were such good friends.

The two of them were snuggled close, their heads touching as they looked out towards the stars. Despite the sweet moment, I couldn't help myself.

"Sofia!" I jogged up to them. Startled, she looked around. But, when she saw who it was, she looked away again.

"Please, Sofia," I said, barely recognizing the pleading note in my voice.

Now, she glared at me and crossed her arms over her chest. "What do you want, Kai?"

"Is Mac okay?" I asked. "I just need to know she's okay."

"What do you care?" Sofia's eyes flashed. She may have been small, but boy, was she intimidating. "You're the reason she was humiliated in front of the whole town."

"Please, let me explain, it wasn't what you think—"

"Dude," Noah said, holding a hand up to stop me. "Maybe just don't."

My heart sank. What was the use? Sofia clearly wouldn't believe anything I had to say. All she knew was that I'd done it – tricked her best friend, humiliated her. She'd seen how I'd put space between Mac and I in the past weeks. And I couldn't tell the truth about why I'd really distanced myself lately, or Click would hurt Mac all the more.

I nodded, looked at the ground. "Sorry, I... just, sorry."

"Mac trusted you." Sofia pointed an angry finger at me, her lip curling in disgust. "She never trusts *anybody*, least of all someone like you. But she took a chance, and look how that went. I can't believe I'm saying this, but she should've listened to Madison."

I frowned at Sofia, more confused than ever. "Madison?"

"Yeah," Sofia said curtly. "She stopped by Mac's house after school yesterday."

Madison had gone to Mac's house? Why?

I shook my head, bewildered. "Wait, what?"

Sofia got up and walked away without answering, clearly done with our conversation. Noah got to his feet, shot me a look that was somewhat sympathetic, then followed her. I stared after them dumbly. What was she talking about?

But, I had no time to dwell on that right now — I needed to confront my teammates about why they'd said it was my idea to get Mac nominated for prom queen. Find out if the person who put them up to that was the same person who was blackmailing me.

I scanned the yard until I caught sight of Zane's signature spiky hair. He was holding up a red solo cup, cheersing everyone who walked by. I made my way over to him and grabbed him by the drunken shoulders.

"Kai," he slurred. "Whassup?"

"Hey, bro, I need you to focus a second. It's important," I said, my voice sharp. "On the bus yesterday, you said it was my idea to set Mac up."

Zane held up a hand for a high five. "Legen-dary, bro."

"No, Zane." I pushed his hand away. "Focus. After I asked you why you thought the prank was my idea, you said 'she said it was.' Who were you talking about? Who's 'she?'"

Zane looked me dead in the eye for a moment. It almost looked like he was completely lucid. Then, his face crumpled and he frowned. "She got us to switch the voting ballots as a team prank. Said it was all your idea."

"Who??"

A slim, dark-haired shape materialized out of nowhere, stepping between Zane and I and effectively interrupting our conversation. Zane winked at me and lurched away without answering.

"Wait," I called out to him. But he didn't, he was long gone towards the kegs.

Fan-freaking-tastic.

"Hey, All Star," Madison cooed and I focused my wild gaze on her.

She was still wearing her cheerleading outfit, though she'd rolled up the hem of her skirt and unbuttoned the top button of her shirt. Her eyes smoldered and her lips were in a perfect pout. She put a delicate hand on my chest and I immediately curled my fingers around hers to remove it.

"What, Madison?" I asked, not bothering to hide the impatience in my tone.

"Why so glum?"

I rolled my eyes and tried to move around her, but she blocked my way.

"You have no reason to be sad, Kai," she simpered. "You're the MVP. The state final winner. The most popular guy in school. You pulled off the world's best prank."

"It. Wasn't. Me." I seethed through clenched teeth.

Madison cocked her head to one side, studied me. "You actually *like* her, don't you?"

"It's none of your business, Madison."

"She won't go to prom with you now, you know. She hates you."

"I know."

"Why don't you go with me, instead?" she purred. "With the *actual* prom queen."

"Frankly, Madison, I'd rather stick my head in a bag of eels." I knew I was being rude, I did. But my patience was wearing thin. I made another attempt to step around her, but she blocked my way with a single stiletto heel.

She laughed lightly, and the sound was like a bell tinkling. "You're so funny, Kai!"

"Madi." I decided to spell it out for her. "I need to talk to Zane right now, we were having an important conversation. Please let me by."

But Madison shook her head and stood her ground. "She never had a chance, you know. All that Anti Prom Queen B.S. wasn't going to work. As if some ginger freak could take my crown."

My blood ran ice cold.

"What did you just say?" My voice was thin and sharp as a blade.

Madison stomped one stiletto and threw her arms in the air. "You heard me. I said, she never stood a chance."

Ginger freak.

The exact words from the Click threat I'd received yesterday evening.

The one threatening to publicly shame Mac's family.

With a picture of Shaun attached.

In his house.

Where, according to Sofia, Madison had gone.

Zane told me "she" had told the team that nominating Mac for prom queen was my idea.

My stomach lurched as the final puzzle pieces clicked into place. I stared down at the simpering girl in front of me with wide eyes. Then, the heat of rage boiled under my skin. Madison? How could she have done this to Mac? Mac had done nothing to deserve any of it.

Fuming, I opened my mouth to tell her off. But then, a thought occurred to me and I froze.

I knew the truth now. I knew who was blackmailing me and torturing Mac. But, I couldn't let Madison know what I knew. She'd go to any lengths to get what she wanted – that much was very clear.

I needed a plan.

Madison batted her eyelashes, mistaking my open-mouthed stare as interest. "So what do you say about prom, Kai? You and me?"

37

MAC

*B*y the next morning, my tears had run dry, and I woke up with a brand new mindset. I wouldn't cry over this any longer. Wouldn't pity myself or wallow.

I could step away from my stupid campaign now. Everyone would laugh at me for a while, but soon enough, Click would dig up some newer, juicier gossip, and I could sink back into relative high school anonymity.

And to think I'd actually believed I could take Click out. Our school ran on Click. Thrived on it, like a pack of hungry wolves tearing into their prey.

They could drag me down, shame me, humiliate me and make me feel small. But they couldn't break me. I meant every word from my Anti Prom Queen platform. Even though it had turned out to be a joke to everyone else, I'd believed in my cause. Believed that I could make Evermore High a better place for others in years to come.

For Shaun.

I'd have to find another way to prepare my brother for the rumors and lies of Evermore High.

And so, with my new mindset, I decided to keep my

phone turned off. Put my headphones on. And I dived head-first into planning my game for the ES Games competition. This was important. A key to my future.

Kai Taylor and Click wouldn't take that from me.

At dinner time, Shaun wandered into my room without knocking. He gave me a gap-toothed grin. "I got you a sandwich."

I set the grilled cheese on my desk, and pulled Shaun in for a spontaneous hug.

"Urgh, gerrof me!" Shaun squirmed, but I held him tight on my lap.

"I love you, Shauney. You know that, right?"

Shaun looked up at me with those big green eyes. He stopped squirming and he nodded slowly. "Love you, too."

I held him for a few moments before he spoke again. "Mac?"

"Yeah, buddy?"

"Why are you mad at Kai Taylor?"

I sighed, deflated. "Sometimes your friends aren't who you think they are."

Madison's chilling words from yesterday shot through my mind — "All I'm saying, Mackayla, is that, sometimes, people keep their friends close and their enemies closer."

Kai had played us. Like the player he was.

But Shaun shook his head vehemently. "Kai is my friend."

"He's not, Shaun," I said.

My little brother's lip wobbled. "You're mean, Mac."

The sad expression on his sweet face broke my heart. "I'm so sorry."

Shaun leaped to his feet, his face turning red. "If he's not my friend, why's he my radio buddy?"

I blinked a few times, not comprehending. "Your what?"

"My radio buddy." Shaun reached into his pocket and held out a walkie talkie. "I gave him my other one so I could talk to him when I'm sad or scared. He said I could talk to him anytime. Mostly, I want to talk about basketball. Nobody in this house knows anything about basketball."

I stared at the little black box like it was a bomb waiting to go off.

"When did you give him that?" My voice was low and quiet.

"A few weeks ago. He came over to see me, and said he couldn't spend as much time with us anymore. But he told me that he would always be my friend. So, I gave him my walkie talkie. He talks to me every day, asks how school was and if I learned any cool new things."

I shook my head, not understanding. Kai had pranked me. He'd pretended to like me.

Why would he go out of his way to keep in touch with Shaun?

"And, he always asks about you," Shaun added.

"Me?" I blinked quickly, trying to absorb all of the information being laid in front of me. This made no sense.

"Yeah. It's sooooo annoying," Shaun said with an impish smile. "I don't want to talk about my sister every single day."

I attempted a smile. "Of course not."

"But he does. All the time. He loves you, I think. Kai is my best friend, Mac. And you shouldn't be mad at him."

And then, before I could stop him, Shaun hit the "talk" button on his walkie talkie. "Agent Taylor, Agent Taylor, come in. I'm in position. Over."

MAC

*S*tatic crackled over the airwaves. I stared at the walkie talkie like it was an object from another planet.

"Roger that, Agent Lafelle." Kai's warm voice filled the bedroom and my heart slammed. "Over."

"What are you doing?" I hissed at Shaun. I attempted to swipe the walkie talkie out of his hand. Failed. "Turn that off."

"Subject is hostile," Shaun whispered into his walkie talkie, backing away from me. "Do you wish to proceed? Over."

"Affirmative, Agent Lafelle. Over."

Shaun tilted his chin up, stood straight and tall like a soldier. "Commencing mission. Over."

"Godspeed, Agent Lafelle. Over and out."

Shaun grinned at me, then ran to the window.

"No, Shaun!" I yelped.

But it was too late. Shaun raised the blinds. Flung open the window.

Across the way, Kai was standing in his bedroom, backlit

by the light. He caught my eye, and then pointed downwards. I crossed my arms over my chest and stared at him skeptically. But, I took a step forward. Looked below.

Outside my window, the entire basketball team stood in a line, dressed in their Panthers hoodies.

Kai signalled to them, and in one, swift motion, they all removed their hoodies to reveal matching shirts with "Vote for the Anti Prom Queen" in big letters. My jaw dropped open in shock.

Then Jordyn stepped into view, clutching her trusty megaphone. "Vote for Mac! Vote for Mac!"

A cheer went up all across my backyard.

From around the corner, Sofia and Noah appeared. They unfurled a huge banner that read *Mackayla for Prom Queen.* Noah put his fingers to his lips and whistled. Loud.

Chase and Dylan arrived next, leading the entire football team. Then Hailey, with half the cheerleading squad. And finally, Trey and his bandmates.

More and more students flocked onto my lawn, cheering and whooping and hollering their support for me. It was surreal to see Evermore High's most elite, most popular, most athletic, on my lawn and gazing up at me.

While I was standing, frozen, in my window. With my mouth wide open, my hair a mess, and not a touch of makeup on my face.

Abby appeared through the crowd. She was directing The Pinnacle's photographer and scribbling notes. She looked up at me and winked.

And above them all, in his window, was Kai.

I grabbed Shaun's walkie talkie. My mouth was dry and I felt lightheaded.

"You did this?" I whispered.

Static crackled in response. Kai held the walkie talkie to his lips and, even backlit by his bedroom light, I could see the way his face fell. He closed his eyes and shook his head. "It was never me, Mac. I never nominated you for prom queen. I was set up. Will you come downstairs? Meet me outside so I can explain?"

Beside me, Shaun clutched my hand. Nodded at me.

Kai had been there for my brother. And, for that reason and that reason only, I decided to give him a chance.

"Okay."

Kai grinned. "Over and out."

39

MAC

*W*hen I stepped outside with Shaun at my heels, everybody cheered. A blush rose to my cheeks and I waved. I was thankful I'd changed out of my pajamas and into my black leggings and a black hoodie. It wasn't every day that you saw your school's entire athletics department in your backyard, along with the coolest band in town.

But, they all faded into oblivion as I locked eyes with Kai. He stood at the front of the crowd. And he was staring at me with more intensity than he ever had.

Despite my anger, my frustration and the feeling of betrayal, my insides flipped.

He took a step towards me.

"Mac, I know what happened," he said quietly. He sighed and gestured to his team, lined up behind him. "Some of the guys on the basketball team nominated you as a prank."

"Why?" My mouth was dry, my voice a croak.

Kai shook his head. "Madison wanted Hailey off the ballot so she got them to help her. She told them it was my idea to nominate you. But, I swear, it wasn't."

I looked around at the basketball team. They were all hanging their heads in shame. Even Zane.

"We're so sorry, Mac," Zane said, his voice more sincere than I'd ever heard it.

I gave him a curt nod, then turned back to Kai.

"I don't understand. If none of this was you, why did you encourage me to campaign? You made me look like an idiot." My throat swelled and tears pricked my eyes.

"Mac, look around you." Kai threw his arms wide. "All of that support for your campaign was real. Nobody but Madison and the guys involved knew about the prank. But the people at school? The people who listened to you? They loved your campaign. People are ready to stop Click's bullying and you gave them hope. Real hope."

I blinked at him, dumbstruck. He took another step forward. Took my hand gently in his. "And I never dated you for any purpose other than the fact that you're amazing."

I wanted to believe him, I really did...

I pulled my hand from his grasp and crossed my arms. Maybe to physically protect my heart. "Why have you been avoiding me, then?"

Kai took a deep breath and held it a moment. Then, he exhaled. "Madison was blackmailing me. It's why I stayed away."

Kai looked at the ground, then back at me. My vision blurred with anger. My gut had been right about that girl.

"That bi—"

"She threatened to come after Shaun publicly." Kai cut me off. "I couldn't do that to you. I knew the entire purpose of your campaign was to protect your brother. And I'd rather you hated me than felt that you failed at doing so." He gave me a tiny smile. "Because I love you. I'd do anything for you, Mac. And I'm so sorry I hurt you."

"I *told* you," Shaun muttered next to me.

I was overcome with emotion. Too many emotions to count. I was blisteringly angry at Madison, I was upset for Shaun, I was bewildered by Kai's words.

But, at that moment, one feeling stood out. My heart pounded and warmth flooded my veins. Kai loved me. He'd believed in my campaign from the beginning and gathered support for me, even when I hated him.

And he'd let me hate him even though it hurt him. All to keep Shaun safe.

I launched myself into Kai's arms. "I love you too, Kai Taylor."

He whipped me off my feet and kissed me deeply.

The crowd went wild.

Kai placed me back on my feet and tucked a strand of hair behind my ear. His eyes melted into mine and my heart skipped a beat.

But a nagging thought bothered me. I stepped away and took his hands. "Is Madison still blackmailing you?"

Kai bit his lip and nodded.

I looked at Shaun, fear forming a knot in my stomach. "What are we going to do?"

Kai gave me his killer smile. And the knot exploded into a pack of butterflies. "Don't worry, Lady Mac. I have a plan…"

"Lady Mac?" I laughed.

"Oh, it's a mountain somewhere in Canada." Kai's lips tugged up at the corners, then he blushed. "You were right, I was running out of ideas."

"Well, it's your lucky day." I squeezed his hands in mine. "Because I like that one."

"And I love you, Lady Mac."

40

KAI

"You look beautiful," I said quietly.

And she did.

Mac wore a midnight blue prom dress that gave her pale skin a luminous glow. Her red hair was woven into an intricate braid crown. She wore chunky silver jewelry and her usual thick black eyeliner. Maybe she didn't look like the stereotypical high school prom queen, but to me, she looked like real life royalty.

"You don't look so bad yourself, Taylor." Mac's eyes gleamed. I glanced down at my charcoal gray suit and navy shirt, and then back at the girl I was head over heels in love with.

She was smiling and my chest felt tight.

"I hope I get to dance with you later." My voice was barely above a whisper.

"The plan's going to work, Kai," Mac replied. "I know it is."

"Let's do this thing." I nodded determinedly. "And whatever happens tonight, it will all be okay... because we have each other."

"Because we have each other," Mac echoed. Static crackled over the walkie talkie. "Godspeed, Agent Taylor. Over and out."

Mac stepped away from her window, and a moment later, her bedroom went dark.

♥

A RED CARPET adorned the steps leading to The Grand Clayton Hotel. The entrance was flanked by huge bunches of gold and silver balloons, and a photographer hovered in the doorway, snapping the pictures of each couple as they stepped into prom.

Lights. Camera. Action.

It was go time.

I stuck my arm out awkwardly, and a scarlet-taloned hand wrapped around it. I took a deep, shaky breath.

Then, Madison and I began to walk.

"It's so beautiful," she cooed, looking around and smiling. Then, she poked me in the side. "Smile, for goodness sake."

I pasted a big, fake smile on my face as we stopped and posed for the photographer. Madison stood in front of me, happy to take the spotlight, while I kept as much distance between our bodies as I could. The photographer snapped away merrily.

It had been a long, tiring week of keeping up appearances.

Since the night outside Mac's house last weekend, I'd been keeping my distance from her in public, making it look like we were well and truly over.

I'd also — grudgingly — accepted Madison's invitation to go to prom together. As much as I'd tried to get out of it, Mac had been insistent on this part of the plan. I hated that most of the school still believed I'd actually set Mac up and humiliated her on purpose, but it needed to be this way.

Basically, Madison had to believe that Mac's Anti Prom Queen campaign was dead in the water. That Mac was no longer going for the win, and that Madson would be the one with the state champion on her arm as her prom date. That way, she'd think she had prom queen in the bag, and we wouldn't be in danger of her sending out a horrible Click blast about Mac's family.

So far, our plan had worked. Click had been uncharacteristically quiet this week.

But, that didn't stop sweat from pricking my forehead as we reached the top step. I held out my hand. "Want me to take a selfie of us before we go in?"

"Sure," Madison purred. She snapped open the clasp on her little purse, and handed me her cellphone.

Bingo.

"Smile," I instructed, angling the phone at us. For the first time since I'd picked her up, my smile was genuine.

The camera flashed as it took the picture and then I dropped her cellphone into my suit pocket. Before she could protest or question why, I led her inside the foyer of the Grand Clayton.

Madison immediately halted, pulled me back. "What the—?"

Her green eyes were wide with horror as she looked around the foyer. I brought a hand to my mouth to hide the irrepressible grin that was creeping over my face.

"Vote for Mackayla!" Jordyn boomed into her megaphone directly into Madison's face. She was resplendent in gold sequins. Beside her were Abby, Sofia, and Hailey, handing out pamphlets.

Around the perimeter of the room, crowds of students were playing on video game stations. Members of the basketball team — wearing their "Vote for the Anti Prom Queen" t-shirts over their suits — were milling around, beckoning people to come and try out the game.

It was the least they could do for Mac after all that had happened. Across the foyer, Zane caught my eye, and shot me a wink. I flashed him a stealthy thumbs-up.

"Just what is going on here?" Madison's voice was shrill as she whirled to face me.

"I'm not sure." I blinked innocently. "Shall we have a look?"

I gestured towards an empty video game station, and Madison stomped towards it, her fists coiled.

"What is the meaning of this?" she screeched at Rob Altman, the unlucky person who happened to be standing beside the empty video game station.

Rob swallowed nervously. "Uh…"

"Allow me," I said smoothly, stepping in between them. Rob shot me a grateful grin, which I returned before twisting to face Madison.

"It's a video game that Mackayla designed," I explained. I held out a controller to her. "Want to play?"

Madison looked at the controller like it was a poisonous snake I'd suggested she cuddle. "I don't play video games."

"Fine." I pressed a button on the controller. "I'll walk you through it, instead. The game is called *Clickbait*. And it's all about saving students from the vicious gossip and rumors that run rampant at their school."

Mac and I had worked hard on the game all week. Well, it was mostly Mac. But I did what I could to help. We'd brought the game to Mr. Vargas and explained our plan, and with his assistance, we'd been able to assemble the video game stations for the prom foyer. Vargas was so impressed, he'd given us both extra credit for the game. Which, combined with my new and improved VGP grades, had brought my overall score in the class to an astounding B+.

Madison's lips puckered. "Is this some kind of a sick joke?"

"Mac is entitled to run her prom queen campaign the way she sees best," I said with a shrug. "Her stance is anti-bullying. Lots of people like it."

Madison looked like she was about to have a full-blown tantrum. Like a toddler. "She wasn't even a real nominee!"

There was a hush over the room at her outburst. She clapped a hand over her mouth, her green eyes wide as she realized what she'd just admitted.

"I know." I looked Madison dead in the eye. "I know exactly what happened. I know you got the basketball team to rig the nominations. You wanted Hailey out of the running so you had a clear path to winning prom queen. So, you had them nominate Mac – a junior, an unknown around school. What you didn't count on was Mac fighting back. And what you *really* didn't count on was people liking what she had to say."

Madison's perfect mouth puckered into a frown and she crossed her arms.

"And when all of that happened," I continued. "You had to pivot to keep your plan afloat. You had to get her to stop believing in herself. So, you came after me. You blackmailed me to force us apart so that Mac would quit and the crown would be yours."

She scowled at me. But, to her credit, she didn't deny it.

"So tonight, you're setting me up?" she guessed, gesturing wildly around the room. "Pretended to be my date to make a laughingstock out of me instead?"

I shook my head. "No, Madison, that's where you're wrong. I stepped away from Mac publicly to stop you from shaming her family on Click. I didn't want to give in to blackmail, but it would've killed her to see her little brother bullied on that app. Tonight, I have no intention of embarrassing you, or humiliating you, or calling you out in front of everyone."

Madison narrowed her eyes, her nose wrinkled. "Why?"

"Because that would mean stooping to your level." I shrugged. "And I'm not going to do that. No underhanded tactics."

Madison's face twisted into a grimace, making her pretty features look almost ugly. "I swear, Kai, I'll—"

"You'll what?" I said flatly. "Send out that nasty, completely uncalled-for Click blast you've got lined up and ready to go?"

Her eyes widened and she fumbled with her purse, realization dawning.

She held out a hand, her face like thunder. "Give me my phone back."

I shook my head. "I'm sorry, Madison. I can't let you hurt Mac's family."

Then, a cool, calm voice spoke from behind me. "It's okay. Give it to her."

41

MAC

"*Mac?*" Kai whirled around to look at me, his dark eyes swirling with confusion.

I nodded. "It's okay. You can give it to her."

Kai looked skeptical as he slowly pulled the phone from his pocket. He held it out to Madison and she snatched it from his grasp. This hadn't been part of our plan. But I knew what I needed to do.

With her phone open in her hands, Madison smirked. Then, she eyed me suspiciously. "You're giving my phone back? Why?"

"Because I want you to have the chance to make the right choice," I said simply. "Otherwise, I'm being a hypocrite. I can't force you not to shame my family, but I can ask to please not do that to my little brother. He doesn't deserve it. You're beautiful, smart, and popular, Madison. You don't need to blackmail and bully others to feel good about yourself. You should want to win prom queen fair and square. That's the only way you can feel good about winning."

Madison gaped at me and I took a deep breath, my confidence building. I offered her a little smile before continuing.

"You're better than this, I know you are. And, like Kai said, our plan was never to shame you or humiliate you. All I ever cared about was keeping my family safe, but I realize now that I can't always be there to protect Shaun. It's not possible. What I *can* do is speak up against bullying and encourage others to do the same."

Madison's eyes narrowed. "But your campaign... you want to win."

"I *did* want to win. Badly," I admitted. "To prove everyone wrong. But I realize now I was focusing on the wrong thing. My becoming queen wasn't going to fix Evermore's bullying problem or Click being vicious. The only way to fix that is to change the narrative. Focus on making Evermore a better place by building people up, not tearing them down."

I pressed a button on my phone and then gestured to Madison's cellphone.

It buzzed in her hand.

Madison looked at the Click blast and her mouth popped open. I smiled, thinking of the words I'd written just moments before.

Madison Albright looks stunning tonight. She'd make a beautiful Prom Queen. #KillClickWithKindness

Madison looked at me. Her face was wary. "You sent this?"

"I did. And it's the truth."

"Why would you do that?"

"To kill Click with kindness. That's how to beat the *Clickbait* game everyone is playing right now. And it's the slogan in the pamphlets people are handing out. I'm no longer campaigning to win prom queen. I don't care who wins. I'm campaigning for a future at Evermore High that's not dictated by endless rumors and lies. And, right now, I'm inviting you to be part of that."

I gave Madison a genuine smile. Because, at the end of the

day, she was just a girl trying to navigate high school. Like the rest of us.

"Ball's in your court, Madison," I said. "You can send out that Click blast about my family. Or, you can take the opportunity to clear Kai's name for something he didn't do."

Kai took a step towards me. "Mac, you don't have to do this. I don't care what people think of me—"

"But I do." I locked eyes with him. "You're a good person, Kai. And I want everyone to know that."

Kai gave me a shaky smile. His eyes were glowing. "I love you, Mac."

"I love you, too." I slid my hand into his, and then turned to Madison. "Whatever you end up doing, just know that I won't hold it against you. But, you have the opportunity to do good right now. And I hope you use it."

Madison stared at me blankly. I had no idea what she was going to do, how she was going to respond. But it didn't matter, because I'd done the right thing. At the end of the day, I still had my mom, my brother, Kai, and all of my friends. They were the ones who mattered the most to me.

I shot her a wink. "Now, excuse us, my boyfriend promised me a dance."

And with that, I led Kai away from Madison and into the main ballroom where prom was taking place. A million fairy lights twinkled, dangling from the various chandeliers. Disco balls spun, shedding shards of mirrored light across the dancefloor.

Prom looked gorgeous. But not as gorgeous as the boy standing in front of me.

Kai wrapped his arms around me, still looking slightly shell shocked. "You didn't have to do that, you know."

I smiled up at him. "I know. But after everything you've done for me, it's only fair."

He bit his lip. "I don't know what I ever did to deserve you, Mac."

Around the room, people were staring. Whispering. Snapping pictures. But I only saw Kai.

"You were you," I responded simply.

My phone buzzed. As did Kai's.

Click.

Kai squeezed my hand. "Moment of truth."

I held my breath as I opened the blast.

Kai Taylor didn't set Mackayla up. He's innocent. I did it. Me, Madison. And I'm sorry. It was mean and heartless, and she didn't deserve it. #KillClickWithKindness

My heart leapt in my throat.

But, before I could process the enormity of what had just happened, my phone buzzed again. And again. And again.

Around the ballroom, everyone was looking at their phones as a stream of Click blasts hit the student body.

Lauren Cowley is a great friend. I appreciate her so much. #KillClickWithKindness

DeAndre Davis is the best bassist ever. So talented. #KillClickWithKindness

I've been in love with Izzy Yang for years. She's the coolest. I've always been too scared to tell her how amazing she is. Until now. #KillClickWithKindness

And the blasts just kept coming. Blasts filled with declarations of love, friendship, support and camaraderie. Students were squealing, gasping, hugging. The sweet sounds of hope and laughter filled the air as positivity spread like wildfire.

Across the ballroom, I noticed Madison standing in the doorway, alone. My eyes met hers, and she offered me a small smile. I beamed back at her.

"Thank you," I mouthed.

She nodded brusquely in response. Then, a hot senior boy

on the basketball team approached her and held out his hand for a dance. She smiled shyly and accepted.

Warmth spread through my body like wildfire. This was a huge step forward. Later tonight, Madison, Jordyn or myself would be crowned prom queen. But, none of that mattered anymore. We were all winners. Every single student who'd stuck up for what was right — fought against Click and bullying, promoted equality, tolerance and kindness — was a winner.

And we didn't need crowns to know it.

Kai grinned at me, shaking his head. "Do you know you've inspired a revolution, Lady Mac?"

"I had to go behind enemy lines to pull it off," I joked.

Kai pulled me closer, cupped my chin with one hand. "Do you regret it?"

And I realized, in that moment, that I didn't regret a thing. I'd always been happy living in relative high school invisibility, waiting for the next phase of my life in the shadows. But, being pulled out of my comfort zone had forced me to stand up and make a difference.

And it had brought me the boy I loved with my whole heart.

"Not for a single second," I whispered and Kai's lips met mine.

MAC

"So, Jordyn Jones." I held an imaginary microphone to her lips. "Have all your hopes and dreams come true this year?"

I was only kidding.

But, Jordyn stole a glance at Dylan, who was playing with the tassel on his cap. She beamed. "They have, actually."

There was an excited buzz backstage in the school auditorium, where hundreds of seniors milled around in caps and gowns, hugging and snapping photos and signing yearbooks. A couple of peaceful, Click-free weeks had passed since prom night, and it was now graduation day for our Evermore High seniors. As Abby was part of the graduating class, I was filling in as school reporter for The Pinnacle.

"What are your plans for after graduation?" I asked Jordyn.

Hailey appeared and threw her arms around her best friend's neck, almost knocking her cap off. "Jordie and I are off to South America this summer to 'find ourselves.' And then, when we get back, she's opening a restaurant with her loverrrr and getting married and having tons of little Ramirez babies and–"

"Shut up, Hailey," Jordyn growled. "It's not like you're following your boyfriend to L.A. or anything."

I turned to Hailey, interest piqued. "I heard Trey and Stonewash Sunrise got a record deal?"

"They did, with a record company in Hollywood. Can you believe it?" She flushed with pleasure. "And I'll be nearby at UCLA. But NOT because I followed him there."

"Noted." I laughed.

"As for me, no babies just yet, Hailey is getting *way* ahead of herself." Jordyn flipped her blond ponytail over her shoulder, genuine pride shining in her eyes. "Dylan is going to culinary school in Denver, and I'm studying Hospitality Management. Hopefully, we *can* actually open our own restaurant one day."

I beamed at Jordyn and Hailey, both absolutely glowing with happiness. "That's amazing!"

Abby and Chase strolled up, hand in hand. Everybody already knew their plans. Even without Click, hot gossip and big news had a way of circulating. Some things would never change.

"Congratulations!" I said to Chase. He'd received full-ride football scholarship offers to Auburn, Ohio State, Texas A&M and Penn State. Penn State was his choice — for the sole reason of being closer to Abby, who would be studying journalism at NYU.

"Thanks." Chase grinned and then he nodded at me. "I'm happy to leave Evermore High knowing you've made this school a better place for everyone."

It was my turn to flush with pleasure. "I wish you guys the best with everything."

As I turned to leave, I saw one more person that I wanted

to speak to. I walked over to Madison, who looked stunning in her cap and gown. I held my hand out for a friendly shake. "Good luck with everything."

Madison took my hand and smiled. "You too, Mac."

It had been a couple of weeks since prom, and nobody even cared about the prom king and queen anymore. The next chapter was about to start, and Madison could walk into it knowing that she had stood up for what was really important.

With a happy heart, I made my way out from backstage and glanced around the crowded auditorium.

"Over here, Mac!" Sofia called. Noah, Sofia and Kai were already seated, and an empty spot next to them was reserved especially for me. I skipped over and took my place, sliding my hand comfortably into Kai's. He smiled at me and I almost melted on the spot.

The auditorium lights dimmed and the school band launched into a rendition of "The Graduation Song." One by one, the graduates took their places on stage.

It had begun.

Principal Potter stood at the podium and addressed the crowd. His speech was touching and sweet, and I couldn't keep a beaming smile from my face looking at the people who'd supported me as they stood on stage.

Halfway through the ceremony, Kai squeezed my hand. He nodded to Abby, who was making her way to the podium to give her Class Valedictorian speech. "That's going to be you next year."

I laughed, and shook my head. "After my speech to Madison on prom night, I feel like I've given enough speeches for one lifetime, thanks."

"I'm so proud of you, Lady Mac," Kai said, holding me close. "And I love you. Maybe even more than basketball."

"I love you, too, Kai Taylor. More than video games."

"Liar." Kai leaned over and kissed me.

I laughed, and nestled my head onto his shoulder. Since getting a B+ in VGP class, Kai was more confident. He believed in himself more, and his smiles were always genuine. He was still friendly with Zane and his teammates, but he'd developed a beautiful new friendship with Noah — much to the delight of myself and Sofia.

These days, we were enjoying double dates, hanging out with Shaun, and playing tons of Mall Zombies. I'd submitted *Clickbait* to ES Games, and had been accepted for a summer internship. Click lived to see another day, but had now become a place for Evermore students to share successes and lift each other up, rather than tear each other down.

In the spirit of progress and making things better, Kai had even sat down with his dad, and the two of them were working on building a better relationship. His situation wasn't perfect, by any means. But together, Kai and I were perfectly imperfect.

And I wouldn't change it for the world.

"Everybody put your hands together for this year's valedictorian, Abigail Murrow," Principal Potter boomed into the microphone. He stepped aside, and Abby took center stage to a huge whoop of applause.

From his place among the graduates, Chase stuck his fingers in his mouth and whistled. Abby winked at him. Then, she cleared her throat, looked out upon the crowd, and smiled.

"If I had to sum up high school in one word, I'd pick electric."

THANK you so much for reading!

If you enjoyed this book, please leave me a review. As a new author, reviews mean everything to me. I appreciate each and every one of them.

CPSIA information can be obtained
at www.ICGtesting.com
Printed in the USA
BVHW031930020421
604058BV00013B/231